MW01617827

fair chase

Also by Travis Mulhauser

Sweetgirl

The Trouble Up North

fair chase

travis mulhauser

New York Boston

This book is a work of fiction. Names, characters, places, and incidents are the product of the author's imagination or are used fictitiously. Any resemblance to actual events, locales, or persons, living or dead, is coincidental.

Grand Central Publishing
Hachette Book Group
1290 Avenue of the Americas, New York, NY 10104
grandcentralpublishing.com
@grandcentralpub

First Edition: April 2026

Grand Central Publishing is a division of Hachette Book Group, Inc. The Grand Central Publishing name and logo is a registered trademark of Hachette Book Group, Inc.

The publisher is not responsible for websites (or their content) that are not owned by the publisher.

The Hachette Speakers Bureau provides a wide range of authors for speaking events. To find out more, go to hachettespeakersbureau.com or email HachetteSpeakers@hbgusa.com.

Grand Central Publishing books may be purchased in bulk for business, educational, or promotional use. For information, please contact your local bookseller or the Hachette Book Group Special Markets Department at special.markets@hbgusa.com.

Library of Congress Cataloging-in-Publication Data

Names: Mulhauser, Travis, 1976– author
Title: Fair chase / Travis Mulhauser.
Description: First edition. | New York, NY : Grand Central Publishing, 2026.
Identifiers: LCCN 2025050008 | ISBN 9781538768013 hardcover |
ISBN 9781538768037 ebook
Subjects: LCGFT: Fiction | Novels
Classification: LCC PS3613.U435 F35 2026
LC record available at https://lccn.loc.gov/2025050008

ISBNs: 9781538768013 (hardcover), 9781538768037 (ebook)

Printed in the United States of America

LSC-C

Printing 1, 2026

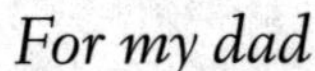

For my dad

fair chase

part I

delos

The night Mr. Baker told me he was going to kill the wolf, I stole his rifle and ran away from foster care for good. I didn't plan it out much beyond the leaving part, because I didn't have the time. I just waited until he was passed out drunk on the back porch and I took that Browning clean off his lap and booked it.

I dumped the rifle in the lime quarry, then made my way up into the forest above the Crow River to see if I could find my people.

The Sawbrooks didn't know they were my people, they had no earthly idea I even existed, but we were kin and they owned six hundred acres of wilderness along the river and I knew they were for the wolf. In fact, the Sawbrooks were the only people I'd even heard of, besides me, that didn't want the wolf dead and gone by yesterday.

The Sawbrooks were not the sort of people that you might expect a runaway to seek out, even if we were related. They were generally thought to be lowlife criminals, and two of them had been shot dead by the police on their own property the summer before. Rhoda Sawbrook got accused of burning up a rich man's boat and killing him, and when the police came to arrest her, she and her husband ran out all guns blazing, got dropped on the spot, and it was about the biggest news story to ever hit Cutler County.

I wasn't afraid, though. I believed they were good enough people because they were for the wolf, and what else was I going to do? Run away with no money, or turn myself in to the police for stealing a firearm and get myself sent back to Woodyard? Shit, the Sawbrooks were nothing compared to the idea of doing a full year in that hellhole.

Woodyard is a prison they like to call a juvenile correctional facility, that way judges can sleep easy at night for sending kids there over nothing. I spent all winter and spring locked up, which felt like a lifetime, but it was also where I first saw the wolf—when we were out on work release clearing campsites at a state park.

It was early in March and it was damp and cold. There were low, gray clouds above the pine trees and we'd driven the prison van up a windy, misty road into the tall forest above the highway.

We were each assigned our own area while the guards patrolled in four-wheelers and generally acted like assholes, heckling us and throwing trash onto our sites just so we'd have to pick it up.

Joe B was the worst. He chucked an empty tin of his chewing tobacco right at my head, but I plucked it out of the air and dropped it on my trash pile in one smooth motion. Then I looked right at him and did a very dramatic yawn.

That got the other Joe, which is what everybody called him—Other Joe—laughing at Joe B.

I knew Joe B would retaliate with some out-of-his-way meanness, which he did. He made me clean the shitters the next time we got work detail, but I didn't care. You got to fight over the inches in your life or you wind up losing miles. That's a quote that somebody said, but it is also my feeling on the matter.

There'd been a storm the night before and we were told to rake leaves and pile the dead branches and debris at our fire-pits. My spot backed right up against a hill and I was dragging a heavy, wet branch from one end of the site to the other when I looked up and saw the wolf not ten feet away.

He was big as hell and no Labrador retriever. He had tall, straight ears and he leaned forward on his front paws and his fur was shaggy and matted and gray-black and wild.

I did not shout for help or scatter off afraid. I just stood with the wolf in front of me, so close I could see the gummy, black edges of his mouth and his big tongue lolling out all loose and wet inside his misty breath. It couldn't have been very long we were face-to-face, but at the same time it felt like it was forever before I heard the four-wheeler making its next lap and coming near. I nodded at the wolf and then he turned and slipped into the pines and the holly brush and he was gone.

I didn't say word one to anybody about that wolf. I didn't tell Carnell or Other Joe, the only guards I halfway liked, and I certainly didn't say anything to the idiots I was locked up with. I wasn't about to share the coolest thing that had ever happened to me with a bunch of solid gold fools, and especially not when there was no upside that I could find to them knowing.

We slept in a big bunkhouse in Woodyard and the whole place stunk like feet and bleach, but I swear when I closed my eyes at night I could see the wolf and smell the damp, piney air that I'd tasted that morning in the woods.

In that time just before you fall asleep, when everything gets fuzzy but not quite a dream, I could see its black eyes shining and its snout all twitchy and wet, and I would remember the way it looked at me and how I looked back and how neither of us flinched.

The only reason I was in Woodyard was because of a bag of cocaine that wasn't even mine. I've never done cocaine a day in my life, but I came home from school one day to find Mrs. Fettering, who ran the foster home I was in at the time, sitting with a sheriff's deputy at the kitchen table.

They put me in cuffs right off and the deputy held up a baggie and said that Mrs. Fettering had found it in my bunk that afternoon.

"That's not mine," I said. "I've never seen that before in my life."

"Then what's it doing in your bed?"

"Somebody put it there, I guess."

"And who would put it there?"

The only other boys in my room were in elementary school and they were good kids and obviously hadn't done it, which left only Mrs. Fettering's daughter, who had done it, I was certain, but when I said her name Mrs. Fettering went off.

Mrs. Fettering had three kids of her own but two were older and out of the house, plus she had the three of us from the county, and she is one of those who everybody is going to side with because she has a good reputation and looks a little bit like a mom from a commercial for a healthy cereal that supposedly tastes good, too. But when it comes down to it, she's not so nice at all.

She got all flushed red and pointed her finger right in my face.

"You ought to be ashamed of yourself, Delos Harris."

I answered her as honestly as I could.

"Well, I'm not. Because I didn't do nothing. And I'll take a piss test right this second to prove it. I've never failed a drug test in my life, and I won't start now."

The deputy said it didn't matter what I pissed if I was selling. That one threw me for a loop.

"Selling?"

The deputy dropped the baggie on the table.

"That's what it looks like to me."

That allegation was pure craziness. If I was dealing drugs, why in the world was I wearing a pair of shoes that were two sizes too small and as ugly as hammered shit?

I swung my feet up on the table for both of them to see and almost went ass over teakettle because I forgot my hands were cuffed behind me. I managed to stay upright just long enough to plead my case, though, which probably didn't do me any favors.

"Drug dealers don't wear shoes like this! These shoes don't even have a brand! They just came in a box that said *shoes*. I get teased over these every day, and you think I'm selling drugs?"

Mrs. Fettering yelled at me so loud about my manners and the rules that I saw the deputy flinch, and then she slapped my feet clean off the tabletop and got up and left the room to go stand in the kitchen and be angry over there.

There was static on the cop's radio and then a voice talking and afterwards the cop told Mrs. Fettering that a transport vehicle was on the way.

"For what? I told you I didn't do nothing!"

The cop pointed at the baggie, like I didn't know exactly what it was we were discussing.

"That looks to be about eight grams of cocaine, son. You're in a foster facility and this is a felony no matter what you claim you aren't doing with it. You know the deal."

I did know the deal. The Fetterings' daughter, Denise, was bad off on drugs and she must have stashed the bag beneath my pillow and forgot about it, or didn't get back to it in time, and then her mom just so happened to be changing out the bedsheets and found it and didn't want to consider the truth, yet alone admit to it. And that's how I got sentenced to six months in Woodyard.

Ms. Mary went with me to the court hearing and spoke on my side. She worked at the county foster facility where I always stayed when I was between other places, which wound up being a lot of my life. Since my mom died, Ms. Mary was the closest thing I'd ever had to a family.

Ms. Mary has dark brown hair and wears glasses with little beads on them and she's always in a sweatshirt and blue jeans, except when she wore sweaters and nice pants if we had to go to court. She is probably the best person I have ever known in my life, and she was pregnant when we went to see the judge.

I remember because I wanted her to be my mom so bad, but I knew she couldn't and I was jealous of her baby. At the same time, I loved the baby because it was hers and if there ever came a time I knew I would protect that baby with everything I had—even if I hated it for being born into a life that I wanted.

Ms. Mary told the judge that I was a good kid and that I didn't belong in prison, and the judge said that Woodyard wasn't a prison. The judge said Woodyard was one of the state's premier resources for wayward youth.

"Well, I don't believe he's wayward, either, Your Honor," she said. "He's just been left out, is all."

"I respectfully disagree," said the judge, and dropped the gavel.

Woodyard is not one of the state's best resources for anything or anybody if you want my opinion on the matter, which nobody did.

The thing is, nothing really happened to me in there like you might think. It wasn't like the movies where there's always some sort of drama or riot going on, and no, I wasn't anybody's girlfriend. Maybe it's like that in other places, but in Woodyard it was just boredom and this feeling in my chest like I couldn't breathe.

That's one thing you don't hear discussed enough in the movies about prison—it's the air inside and how heavy it is and how it settles into your blood like poison. You got to be careful breathing the same air as idiots, or I swear you can catch their foolishness and bad ideas like a disease.

In the end, Woodyard was six months of labor and schoolwork and dinners they poured into heating pans out of aluminum drums. It was fences and razor wire and sadness and fear, and the day they took me back to Cutler in the transport van I swore I'd die before I ever returned.

The second time I saw the wolf was late in June. I was with my new foster family, the Bakers, and I was in their backyard pulling weeds when I felt the tiny hairs on the back of my neck stand on end.

I wheeled around and saw him, motionless, on top of a little rise by the tree line about fifty yards away. He had the same matted, gray-black fur and we stared at each other just like we had the first time.

He didn't linger very long. He must have heard or smelled something, because I saw him twitch, just slightly, and then he darted off into the dark space between the pines and I sat there for a good two minutes with my heart skipping in my chest.

I stayed awake until damn near dawn that night, hoping to catch a glimpse of him out my window, or to hear him howl somewhere off in the trees.

I didn't see or hear him, though, and I started to wonder if maybe I'd made the entire thing up. I knew for a fact that I saw a wolf when I was locked up, but Cutler is two hours away from Woodyard, by car, and as far as the Bakers' yard was from the tree line it really could have been a dog or some fucked-up-looking coyote that I'd seen that afternoon. And I do have a known history for imagination.

When I was a kid and my arm used to fall asleep I sincerely believed I was growing superpowers. I'd get that funny, tingling feeling from elbow to fingertips and be convinced I was in the process of developing flame-throwing capabilities, or maybe my arms were becoming wings that would suddenly grant me the ability to fly. I would spend hours thinking on that—wondering which talent would be mine and whether I would use it for good or for evil.

I know most kids have imaginations, but I took mine to entirely different levels. It wasn't just the superpower stuff. A lot of it had to do with the Sawbrooks.

My mom told me we were related when I was little, and I spun that off in so many directions in my head that I can't remember what I've made up and what I've read about or heard.

The Sawbrooks are known all over Cutler County. They go back to the beginning of this town and, while most people dislike them, my mom straight-up hated them.

I remember my mom pretty well. She had long, dark hair and she smoked a lot of cigarettes, and we always rode around together in other people's cars and whenever we passed the river she would point to it and say the Sawbrooks were our kin and that the property they owned should have been ours too, but that it wasn't because they were bastards and sons of bitches.

Mom didn't know who her mom was, but she said her daddy was a Sawbrook and that his family didn't want her and that was why her mom dumped her at an orphanage and bolted. If she knew her mother's name she never told me, and I never knew anything about her or where she went.

My mom came up in the orphanage at the Catholic church—Sisters of the Redemptive Light—but she never was adopted and ran away when she was thirteen. Then she got pregnant and had me a little while later.

I never saw her do drugs that I can remember, but I know she died of an overdose because I looked her up on the internet and there was an article about it in the *Cutler County Herald*. They found her in an abandoned barn on Foster Road and there was a little picture of her face beside the story, but it was small and fuzzy and was one of those photos that looked like it could have been anybody at all.

I do remember we lived in lots of different places with lots of different people and she slept a lot and was sick all the time and sometimes she just disappeared for a while. I spent a lot of time by myself just wandering around and wondering about life. Then she was gone forever and I was in the county system. I think I was about seven years old at the time, maybe eight.

I didn't claim my Sawbrook heritage right away. Mostly, I sat around county hoping to be adopted, and I knew the Sawbrooks were considered dangerous and not the sort of family that anybody would choose to be associated with.

I kept my bloodline on the down-low for about two years, right up until the moment I decided to stop waiting for some magic family to save me, and put some use to the kin I did have.

It started because this motherfucker, Randy, kept stealing my Little Debbies and one day I just blurted that I was a Sawbrook and that he would have hell to pay if he crossed me again.

We got Little Debbies every Tuesday and Thursday night because the Kiwanis Club donated them and it was the highlight of my week, until Randy came along and ruined it. He was too big and too mean for me to mess with on my own, so I told him that my people would come flying out of the hills the second I said the word and string his ass up on the flagpole in Memorial Park downtown. I told him that if he so much as breathed on another one of my Swiss Rolls it would be the last breath he ever took.

There was no grand plan to it. No strategy whatsoever. I just wanted my rightful dessert.

Randy said if I was a Sawbrook, then why was my last name Harris, and what was I doing in county and not living out on their property?

They were good questions, and if I hadn't responded it wouldn't have gone a single step further. Randy would have just laughed and made fun of me while he continued to stuff himself on my desserts. Instead, I came up with an answer on the spot that surprised even me.

"My mama was a Harris, but her daddy was a Sawbrook and after she died the court wouldn't let me stay with them because of how dangerous they are, and all they've done ever since is try to get me back and bring me home."

"Bullshit."

"Try it and see."

Randy was a year older and a lot bigger, but something in my story gave him just enough concern because he ran off to ask Big Mike if it was true.

Big Mike was fifteen and he had his nickname for a reason. He sort of ran things in the facility and he played along without me having to say so much as a word to him. Told Randy it was true and that he better watch his back.

I think Big Mike was just bored and wanted to mess with Randy, but from then on if anybody got an extra dessert it was because Randy offered me his, or I kicked mine over to Big Mike as tribute.

Dudes came and went out of county, but my story stayed with me and the longer it went on the easier it was to pass off. I did some research to fill in the blank spots and I came to know a lot about the Sawbrook family and used what I could in any way that would serve me.

For instance, one thing the Sawbrooks are known for is being expert swimmers. They all worked in the lakes and rivers being smugglers and running moonshine, and none of them had ever died a water death—not even ones that were in terrible shipwrecks or were lost out in storms for days on end.

They were legendary for it, yet I couldn't swim a lick. I'm afraid of the water is the truth of the matter, but when we did anything at the beach with the county I just lounged in the sand and soaked up the sun and nobody even considered the fact that I was scared to get in the water and so nobody teased me or ever took a run at me over it.

People in county knew of Buckner Sawbrook, because he was a badass who'd done a lot of crazy things and fought in a war, and because he wasn't old enough to already have been forgotten.

I made up all kinds of shit that me and Buckner did together, and sort of made it like he was my mentor and I was his protégé. I'd tell these stories about the two of us having adventures and escapades together, and sometimes I'd just steal something from a TV show and put my own spin on it, and people seemed to go along with it more often than not.

People might judge me for all the stories I told, but let me ask you this—how much of your life did you hit the ground running with? How many of your stories were provided to you, and how much do those stories help hold together the stray parts of your life that you might not otherwise have an explanation for?

You know how many times at school I heard somebody say "My daddy did this" or "My mama did that"? You know how many kids claim they had family on the *Mayflower*, or that their grandaddies and uncles were heroes in some World War? And how many of those stories are actually true? You don't think some bullshit got spread around over the years, with different people claiming different things? And how come nobody ever says they're related to the Pilgrims that put the diseases in the blankets or shot up the Indians for no reason? There's a helluva lot of people on the *Mayflower* that seem to have up and disappeared the moment the bullets started flying. And why should Randy get my Little Debbies, just because I was smaller than him? Yeah, I could have fought back, but I'd seen Randy beat down plenty of kids and the only thing I was going to get for trying to defend myself with my fists was a bloody nose to go with my no-dessert.

So yeah, I made stuff up. Then I did some research and made more stuff up. Not everybody believed me about everything I said, but I reached a point where in the foster system and juvenile correction facilities it was pretty much established that the Sawbrooks, my family that I'd never spoken to in my life, that didn't know I existed, would murder anybody that tried me without a second thought. And I don't apologize for that at all.

I crossed paths again with Big Mike about two years after he helped me get the whole thing started. He was coming out of some military training school, and I was just back from a few months with the Jessups.

The Jessups were an overly religious family that took on temporary foster kids just so that they could save their souls and then sent them back to the county. The Jessups didn't allow music or dancing or television, but they had great food and comfortable beds and I would never have accepted Christ as my personal Lord and Savior had I known that was all they were after. The only reason I let Christ into my heart was because I thought that's what I had to do to get adopted by the Jessups, but it turned out it was the exact opposite, and as soon as my ninety days were up, they were hauling me back to the county to exchange me for some other unsaved soul.

I was sad to be back inside, but it was good to see Big Mike. He was about to be discharged from the system altogether and said he was planning to join the Marines, and asked if I could make up a backstory for him.

"How do you mean?"

We were outside in what they called the recreation area—which was a grass field surrounded by a fence. We were sitting at the picnic table and taking rips off a cigarette Big Mike had snuck in. We'd pass it beneath the table and exhale all incognito into a sploof, which is an empty toilet paper roll with a dryer sheet on the end. Big Mike always had one of those at the ready, somehow.

"Like when you made that one up about the Sawbrooks," he said. "How'd you do that?"

"I don't know. I just wanted Randy to stop stealing my Little Debbies so I made something up that I thought might work."

Big Mike ducked down to blow a line of smoke and when the smell of tobacco and lavender drifted over I reached beneath the bench for both the cigarette and the sploof.

"No, but you went deep with it. You did research and learned things, and when you would tell people, you were so slick with it. I've never seen anybody lie that good."

Big Mike meant it as a compliment, but it bothered me some, too. I didn't want to be a liar so much as I wished certain things were true. I took my turn and passed back to Mike.

"I have Sawbrook in me for real, so I just built on that. I took a grain of truth and worked it into something more. But why would you need a story? Nobody's stealing your desserts. You're Big Mike."

He was big, too. He was about six four and 240 pounds by then, and it wasn't fat or chiseled muscle he got from a weight room. He was just born big and country strong and I couldn't imagine him being afraid of anything in the world.

"The ladies, dude. I need something to tell them. I can't be Big Mike, the orphan. That shit's depressing."

"Some girls like it."

"I don't want those girls."

"What kind of girls you want?"

"Don't get me wrong, I'm not picky. I'm just saying it'd be nice to have something else in my toolkit. You know what I mean?"

We passed back and forth a few more times and then Big Mike put the cigarette out on his tongue and dropped the butt in his pants pocket. He'd chuck the butt and the sploof over the fence later, but I could tell he didn't want to go in just yet. I could tell he was serious about me helping him.

"You want to make up a family for you?"

"I just need something, man. I need something to say to a

girl when she asks me about myself. I'm going to be a Marine. I'm going to do all sorts of badass shit eventually, but I mean between now and then. You know, so I can get some action before boot camp."

"Like, maybe you're joining the Marines because your daddy was a Marine and he got killed in a war?"

"Yes! Exactly like that, dude. That's what I'm talking about. 'Cause my real daddy is just a piece of shit that didn't want me. What war?"

"What?"

"What war did he die in?"

"I don't know, maybe one of the Iraq ones? There was a couple of them. Just google it and see what timeline fits."

"What would his name be?"

"Whatever you want."

"Just make it up?"

"Sure, why not?"

"How'd you get it to stick so good, though? Man, I'm telling you, I met this dude in the training school that was telling me this story about a kid that he met in county that used to run drugs into Canada for the Sawbrooks, and halfway through the story I realized he was talking about you."

"I never said I ran any drugs."

"Exactly! He put his own bullshit on top of yours and spun it off in an entirely new direction. But you planted the seeds down in a way that they took root. You've got a gift."

"You're the only one that knows the truth."

"Still?"

"Wait," I said. "I got it."

"Got what?"

"Your dad's name was Mike. Everybody called him Big Mike and you were Mike Jr., but then he died in the war and that's why everybody started calling you Big Mike, because you became the man of the house."

"See? That's what I'm saying. How did you do that?"

"I don't know. I didn't even think about it. I just said it."

"But it's the way you said it."

"How did I say it?"

"Like it was the God's honest, absolute truth. Shit, I believe it myself."

"You could just try being honest."

"Maybe, but I'm saying if that doesn't work it's good to have a backup."

The funny thing about that conversation was that I lied to Big Mike about lying. I did care about the stuff I said. I didn't make everything up all carefree and willy-nilly. That's how it started, but the longer it went on and the more I learned about the Sawbrooks, the more I wanted it to be real.

In my heart I've always wished I had a family, and sometimes, if I'm being perfectly honest, I let myself believe that I did.

Turned out I did see the wolf at the Bakers'. The proof came quick, too. The next morning, one of the neighbors found a barn cat behind their house with its guts all stretched out across the yard and bloody clumps of fur scattered in the grass.

Mr. Baker told me about it at dinner. He said the people

were near certain it was a wolf and not a coyote because of how big the tracks were, but that the people in that house were not the kind who would call in the authorities and ask them to come by to launch some sort of investigation. Mr. Baker said those people had far bigger concerns than a barn cat.

Mrs. Baker had excused herself to go to the bathroom, but she must have come back while Mr. Baker was talking because he stopped all of the sudden in the middle of his story, and when I turned around I saw her standing in the doorway.

I could tell she was upset, right away. Very upset. Her face was drained of color and nobody spoke and the mood in the whole house went cold. I waited for something to happen, but Mrs. Baker just stood there while Mr. Baker's mouth hung open like somebody had popped a hinge in his jaw.

I listened to the kitchen noises—the whir of the fan above the stove and the plunk of water droplets hitting the sink. There was still sunlight through the windows above the counters and a swipe of orange in the sky where the sun was setting over the pines. Mr. Baker tried to change the subject by saying what a nice day it had been outside, and that was when Mrs. Baker turned and ran away upstairs.

Mr. Baker followed after her, and neither came back down for the rest of the night.

I was pretty happy at the Bakers'. Happy enough, at least. Mrs. Baker was kind and she was a good cook and my daily chores were reasonable and mostly outside.

Mr. Baker signed me up for Little League and drove me to

practices and sat in the stands to watch my games and afterwards I felt that he was vaguely proud of me and impressed by my play. I played center and batted third and I was as fast as anybody in the league and stole bases whenever I wanted and had not once been caught.

Mrs. Baker did not drive me anywhere or come to my games, but that was because she never left the property. She ordered her groceries for delivery and was mostly on her computer during the day watching auctions on eBay and reading news stories that made her angry and afraid. Sometimes, she'd go outside and work in the garden, but she always came back in before long, talking about how tired she was, and then she'd lay down in her room upstairs and sleep.

I knew I was there because Mrs. Baker had wanted me and that Mr. Baker had gone along out of love for his wife. Mr. Baker treated me well, though, and did not blame me for my presence the way some other less willing types had in the past.

There were no pictures of other children in the house, but there was a sadness that hovered above Mrs. Baker and I thought she had probably lost a baby once, or maybe tried to have one but never could.

This reminded me of the story of Mabel Sawbrook, who was famous in lumberjack times for murdering a man, an attacker, by shoving a fire poker through his nuts—that's real, you can read about it—and you can also read about how Mabel had a stillborn daughter that she called Ellerbee, and that the main creek on their property was named after that baby. That's how history works. Most things got names for a reason, and once you learn about those reasons you start to understand the world.

Mabel's hurt was so big she called it a creek that could run on into forever, but I think Mrs. Baker just tried to replace what she'd lost and that it wasn't working, because something in that wolf story sent her spiraling.

She didn't come down the morning after she got upset, or the next day after that. She stayed locked up in her room and the whole house started to feel heavy and sad. Mr. Baker started staying longer at work, but I kept myself busy looking for tracks.

The going was pretty slow at first. There was trampled brush around where I'd seen the wolf behind the house, but the only tracks I found were outside the barn where Mr. Baker said the cat got killed, and they weren't much to look at.

I'd looked up wolf tracks on the internet, but the ones online were obvious and off by themselves on flat ground, while the two I found were all crooked and mixed in with the grass around them. They were big, though. I could tell that much when I stretched my hand from the back of one marking to the front and could not cover it completely.

I stomped the tracks out and moved closer to the barn. There was loud music playing inside and two cars up on cement blocks and machine parts scattered around the grass. The music was a bunch of loud, violent screaming and screeching guitar—the type of stuff the metalheads in Woodyard would have loved—and I scanned the ground around me as quickly as I could.

There were a few clumps of orangish fur caught up in an engine part, and inside the cylinder of that part is where I saw the cat paw all pale and stiff with dried blood and separated clean from the rest of the cat. It startled me, but not as much as when I heard a shout and a clicking sound and looked up to see a man in blue jeans and his bare chest holding a shotgun. The man lifted the gun in my direction and I ran for the rise and did not stop until I'd made it back to the Bakers' gravel drive.

I kept to the river after that. The Crow is big and wide and there's spots of fast current and white water, but it also has long, lazy bends and gentle stretches where the water pools deep. It comes out of Long Lake to the north and connects the resort's two separate locations.

One half of the resort is built up where the Crow empties into Lake Michigan, then it spreads upriver and in total it's two golf courses, a marina, a hotel and stores and restaurants and mansions and condos. Harbor North takes up damn near all the Crow River, which meant there was only but so many spots that the wolf could actually be. Two, to be exact.

The first was the state land at Crooked Tree Park, where campsites and hiking trails sat between the river and the public beach. The second was the far end of the Crow where all the construction runoff had turned the river into swamp—or at least that's what Ms. Mary said had happened. She was one of those that was opposed to the resort and had a lot of bumper stickers about it on her Toyota.

I started with the campsites and hiking trails, since that's the same sort of area as where I'd first seen the wolf.

Crooked Tree wasn't emptied out like the one in Woodyard, though. There were plenty of campers and no tracks or markings, so I pushed downstream past the resort and the falls where the river runs fast and drops. Then I made my way through the beat-up, run-down houses, where some locals still lived and there was nothing anywhere I looked until I went a little farther and crossed the river to the west bank.

The water at that end of the river was gritty and warm. I stripped down to my shorts and my bare feet sunk to the shins in the clay bottom the moment I stepped in. It was hard to push through all that muck and mess and there were a few times that I lost my balance and almost went under. Luckily, there was a downed birch in the water close to the other side that I finally latched on to, and I used that to pull myself to shore.

There were fat black flies and mosquitoes and some steady insect humming in the tall grass between the river and the trees. The land was low and flat, but it rose quickly into the rocky hills off the river, and just when I started to think that those hills were a place that a wolf could bed down I saw tracks in the mud.

The prints were wide and deep and they were clear as day compared to the ones I'd spotted in the field outside the barn. Now I could see the heel as something separate from the claws, and the tracks sunk down deep in the mud, and that was when I first realized how big the wolf probably was. I'd seen him from a distance, but even up close I hadn't really been able to put everything together in my mind.

I only saw the wolf in fragments when I was in Woodyard. I could remember the gnarly fur and the way he leaned forward on his paws. I'd seen the tall ears and dark eyes, but they were all pieces that didn't fully snap together in my mind until I saw those clear, deep tracks in the mud.

The tracks led off the river and I stomped them all out as I followed them up into the forest, and when the tracks ran out there was still trampled brush and I followed those markings until I came to a big, mossy rock that sat high and jagged above the grass.

The markings split in two directions at that rock. One went upstream, and the other headed higher into the woods. I figured the wolf was staying overhead in the hills, and that when he came down he either drank there or went upstream and followed the woods that looped around the river and stretched clear to where I stayed on Cut Road.

I planned to go back the next day and to walk as high as I could into the forest, but Mr. Baker had other plans. Mr. Baker said we were putting up a fence.

For the first time since his wife had locked herself in her bedroom, he mentioned Mrs. Baker, too. He said she was having a spell and that we needed to put something solid in the ground to have between her and the wolf to help her feel safe. He said we'd get started at seven a.m. sharp and I asked him if I could get up at six and go for a run before we worked.

"A run?"

"Yes, sir. I'm trying out for football in the fall."

This wasn't a full lie. I'm a badass wide receiver. I'm fast and I'll catch anything and I don't get afraid of being tackled over the middle, either. I was going out for football that year, but the run was just so I could go down to the river and stomp out any tracks the wolf might have left, because I didn't want the wrong people to notice them.

"If you're ready to work at seven, and don't get too tired, then hell yes you can get up and run. Good for you, Delos."

So that's what I did. I got up and ran to the river and I stomped out anything I saw that looked like wolf. Then I ran back to the Bakers and worked. It was no joke, either. Putting up a fence is hard work, and don't let anybody tell you otherwise.

Everything was delivered in stacks at the end of the driveway and it took us three days to get it in the ground. We dug postholes, snapped the panels together, and then pounded them into the dirt.

Mr. Baker would pick up fast food and we would eat on the porch steps and drink pop out of the paper cups that came with our lunches and then we would gather up our energy and get right back to it.

Yes, eventually I stole Mr. Baker's rifle and ran away, but that was just because we did not see eye to eye on the wolf. Otherwise, I liked him. I respected him, too. I admired how much he loved his wife and how hard he was willing to work to help her, because he damn near broke his back putting that fence in.

Mr. Baker was so beat-up he wound up sleeping on the couch so he wouldn't have to mess with the stairs, and the morning after we finished, he asked me if I could fix Mrs. Baker's breakfast and run it upstairs myself.

I made butter toast and cereal and poured Mrs. Baker a glass of juice and walked it all carefully to her room on a tray. I knocked softly on the door but Mrs. Baker did not answer, and Mr. Baker called out from the couch downstairs.

"Just go on in," he said.

I pushed the door open slowly. The bedroom air was heavy and stale, and somehow it smelled both rotten and sweet. Mrs. Baker was lying in bed, staring at the far wall.

There was a TV on the dresser but it was turned off and there was a big window that looked out at the yard but she was turned the other direction and I set her tray down on the nightstand, and that was the third time I saw the wolf.

The window looked out on the backyard and the new fence. There was mist above the grass and bands of light that striped the field between the house and the pines and I saw the wolf trotting along the same rise where I'd seen him the second time.

My heart went still and I watched him until he dissolved into the distance and then the wind came and rustled the brush and bent the tall grass in the field.

Mr. Baker took a bunch of Advil for his back and told me that Mrs. Baker was going to be feeling better now that the fence was up and that we were going to grill out that night for dinner to celebrate. He said he was going to be busy running errands during the day, but that I should rest up because I'd earned it.

"And if Mrs. Baker comes downstairs before I get home, just let her know you're glad to see her and that I'll be home soon. Tell her to let you know if there's anything she needs."

"Yes, sir."

Mr. Baker left, but Mrs. Baker did not come downstairs. I got on the internet to do a search on wolves in northern Michigan and that was how I found a link to the livestream for a town hall meeting at the VFW. Above the link it said "Update on Wolf Sightings." I clicked it.

The VFW was packed with people sitting on folding chairs and there were tons of people in the live chat, too, and before it even got started I could feel how angry everybody was at the wolf. The chat was all people posting links to horrible stories about wolf attacks and talking about how dangerous wolves were, and even on the livestream you could feel how tense it was in the VFW.

The people leading the meeting sat at a table on a small stage. There was a farmer, a man in a dress shirt and sport coat, and then I saw Lucy Sawbrook wearing a hat that said RANGER. There was an empty seat between Lucy and the last person at the table—a man with a nameplate in front of him that said TOWNSHIP COUNCIL.

I should have figured that Lucy would be involved with the wolf, being a ranger with the Michigan Department of Resources, but I honestly wouldn't have guessed she'd be so much on the wolf's side.

The farmer was against the wolf and he received the loudest applause. He spoke about his livestock and how he was going to lose all this money if his chickens got ate. Lucy spoke next, but she got booed so loud that she didn't speak very long. She said there was no real proof there was a wolf in the area, and that for her money it was more likely that everybody was freaking out over nothing.

"And if there is a wolf, I guarantee you that it is no threat to anybody in this room. Point blank, period."

That's when the booing got so loud that she just gave up and crossed her arms over her chest. I could feel how pissed she was through the screen.

The man in the suit coat said if the federal government came in, then it would cost everybody money and set the entire area back years and that families would go broke and lose their homes.

That man received a lot of applause, but not quite as much as the farmer.

The township council man kept saying things like, "I think most of us here are in agreement." Or, "I think there's a reasonable majority here on this issue."

Then somebody in the audience shouted, "What are you going to do about it, then?"

That question got a big cheer, but the township man's answer was not very popular. They booed whatever he said almost as loud as they booed Lucy, and then somebody said they had a rifle at home and knew exactly what they were going to do about the wolf.

People went crazy for that, and then a woman in the crowd stood up and said she was concerned about her cats.

"Which isn't to mention babies and toddlers," she went on. "Is it even safe for little ones to be playing outside right now? I know my grandbabies have been indoors the last two days and driving everybody up a wall. It's no good for them in the summer to be cooped up, but we got a damn wolf roaming around the woods and we are not putting our little ones out there as bait. I am in full favor of getting our best hunters out there to take care of this thing the only way they know how."

Everybody started clapping for the lady, and that was when Buckner Sawbrook stood up.

I'd been telling stories about Buckner for years. I always described him like he was damn near a Yeti, but if anything I'd undersold his size. He was easily the biggest dude in the VFW. He had huge shoulders and a big, square head and he stood straight and spoke loud.

"First of all, wolves don't eat kids unless you're reading a damn fairy tale. That's just not a thing that happens, so you can let them grandbabies out of doors, Ms. Michaels, I promise. Second, all due respect, fuck your cats. If you're that worried, keep them in. If you let them out and they get eaten, well, maybe they shouldn't have been so coddled all these years."

That one got people going wild, both in the VFW and on the chat. People were talking about how Buckner was an alcoholic and that his views were irrelevant and not welcome in a public forum. Somebody else said criminals couldn't vote so it didn't matter what he said, and then somebody in the VFW said Buckner should shut his mouth and go somewhere and get drunk.

Buckner didn't react, though. He just waited for the crowd to calm down and then went on.

"I lost my dog here recently. Harold. Good boy, great boy. Best dog I ever owned, so I understand about pets, I truly do, but let's be honest, you keep your cats indoors anyway, Ms. Michaels, and even if you didn't we can't go around making up rules about what animals get to live and which ones get to die. What if I got a pet mouse and I said, 'Ms. Michaels, your cats are a threat to my mouse, so I'm going to come over to your house and shoot Conrad and Minny.' Is that okay?"

Ms. Michaels started shrieking.

"That is a threat! Everybody here heard it!"

She was stating her case to all of the crowd now. She turned in a little half circle and kept going.

"Buckner Sawbrook knows the names of my cats and is stalking me!"

Buckner didn't shout, but somehow his voice was even louder than hers.

"I'm not stalking you, Ms. Michaels. Shit, we're Facebook friends. All you do is post about those two cats. I know Conrad just had a birthday, for instance, so happy birthday to him."

Buckner sat down and it was like somebody had set a torch to some dry kindling and set that meeting on fire. It was all shouting from there on in and before long the people at the table dispersed into the crowd and groups formed around them and then the feed cut out, and I had never felt so much like I wanted to be a Sawbrook as I did at that moment.

I had a feeling like maybe I did belong in that family, and that all the Sawbrook pride I'd been lying about had somehow come from a place that could turn out to be real.

Mr. Baker put burgers on the grill that night and set out a big spread of potato salad and chips and pop, and then he went upstairs and tried to get Mrs. Baker to come downstairs for dinner.

He was up there for half an hour at least, probably longer, and when he came back down he looked like he'd been crying. That man loved his wife something fierce, and I felt bad for him while I sat there and ate. He didn't have any appetite, but told me to go ahead.

"No sense in this going to waste," he said.

"Yes, sir."

"You done a good job on that fence, Delos," he said. "I appreciate your help."

"You're welcome, sir. I didn't mind the work at all."

"You can call me Chuck," he said.

"Sir?"

"Chuck is my name, and this isn't any place for a boy to be right now. I'm going to call the county tomorrow, and in the meantime I'm going to sit out here with my rifle and if I see that goddamn wolf I'm going to kill it."

Mr. Baker got up then and he walked to the storage shed and came back with a hunting rifle and a six-pack of beer he must have plucked out of the mini fridge in the shed.

He set the rifle down beside his chair and opened his beer and drank, and after I finished eating I cleaned up the food and did the dishes and when I looked back outside there were already three empties on the ground and Mr. Baker had cracked his next one open. I got a feeling right then that if Mr. Baker got half a chance, he was going to kill the wolf.

I waited up until just after midnight. I put my head beneath my pillow and I closed my eyes and I was so afraid that I was going to hear that rifle shoot that I made myself sick to my stomach.

Mr. Baker never shot the rifle, though, and as soon as I was certain that he was passed out asleep, I took it and I ran.

jewell

Jewell was the first to see the boy. She spotted him through the mist and morning fog in the field between her house and the forest and she was struck by how still he stood among the tall grass and chicory—how arrow straight and assured he seemed.

She was on the front porch, drinking coffee, and whispered to her brother, Buckner, beside her.

"Do you see that?"

"See what?"

She tilted her mug toward the field.

"That."

Buckner leaned forward. Peered into the dawn.

"Who is that?"

"I have no idea."

"What does he want?"

"How would I know what he wants if I don't know who it is?"

Jewell raised her hand in a half wave. The boy returned the gesture but did not come forward.

Buckner drank from his coffee.

"He's not moving."

"I can see that."

"He's making me nervous."

"It's just a boy. He looks thirteen, maybe fourteen."

"Those can be the worst ones."

Now Jewell motioned with some emphasis—more of a command than a greeting—and he finally stepped forward.

"Thank God," said Buckner. "That was creepy, the way he was just standing there."

"Poor thing is probably just frightened. He's had to be out in the woods all night. The sun's not even up above the pines."

"But what's he doing on our property?"

"That's a good question."

"Which is why I asked it," said Buckner. "Where's Lucy?"

"She left for work."

"Already?"

"I think so. Why?"

"'Cause she's good in situations like this."

"What kind of situation is this? 'Cause I've got no idea."

"I don't know. You've got a wayward minor without adult supervision. The situation is developing. It's the sort of thing she knows how to handle as a park ranger. They have trainings that apply to this sort of thing."

The boy arrived at the base of the porch steps and glanced around, seeming to take in the land. Finches were chattering in the canopy, and in the far distance there was a blue cut of the Crow River. There were dewdrops in the grass beyond the reach of the shadows from the roof, and a hawk turned a high half circle above the pines.

Finally, the child spoke.

"Good morning."

Jewell looked at the boy, puzzled.

"Good morning. Can we help you with something?"

"Maybe so, yes."

"What's your name?"

"My name is Delos Harris."

"Well, I'm Jewell Sawbrook and this is my brother—"

"I know who you are."

The boy pointed at Buckner.

"That's Buckner Sawbrook and I know who your sister Lucy is, too. I've been knowing about you for all of my life."

Buckner tilted his head at the boy.

"Really?"

"Yes, sir."

"Can I ask you how?" Jewell said. "Or why?"

"Because I'm your blood kin, through my mother, Tina Harris. She died when I was eight years old but told me who I was and where I came from when I was little."

Buckner turned to Jewell. Spoke quietly.

"Tina Harris was the one that—"

"She died in a barn on Foster Road," said Delos. "Of a drug overdose. It was in the newspaper."

"I remember that," said Jewell.

"So do I," said Delos.

Buckner leaned back in his rocking chair now. Studied the boy. He wore his brown hair cut close and there was a smattering of pimples and freckles across his forehead and he was at the age where he seemed to flicker, by the moment, from a boy to a man and then back again.

"I'm pretty confused right now," said Buckner. "I'm just going to go ahead and say that out loud."

Jewell was fairly certain the child was a runaway and spinning some sort of lie about who he was in an attempt to win their favor.

Their cousins on their father's side were all grown and moved away and all their children were accounted for. They were not close with their father's side, in part because their father himself hadn't been. The children all bore their mother's surname and while it was possible a Clark had slipped through the cracks, it seemed unlikely. Meanwhile, both their mother's siblings had died young and did not have children. At least not that their mother had known of, and Rhoda would have known. Rhoda knew everything there was to know about the Sawbrooks, or at least it had always seemed that way to Jewell.

"Do you need help, Delos? Are you lost?"

"I'm not lost, and I might need help, but that's not the reason I'm here. The reason I'm here is because I know where the wolf is, if you all want to find him."

lucy

Lucy's phone buzzed all morning. Buckner and Jewell were lighting her up about the boy and the wolf, but she had no idea because she kept her cell in her glove box on Do Not Disturb. Lucy hated her phone, especially when she drove.

She was on the highway headed south because Ralph, her boss, had requested an off-the-books meeting at a bowling alley in West Branch. It was nearly a two-hour drive for Lucy, and slightly further from Ralph's office at the state capitol in Lansing. He surely wanted to discuss the wolf, and she was certain that they were not going to see eye to eye on the proper course of action.

There hadn't been a gray wolf in the pines of northern Michigan for over a hundred years, but it seemed likely that one had slipped out of the federal preserve in the Upper Peninsula that winter, crossed the ice, and come south.

There'd been scattershot reports of howling on the northeast coast all spring, and talk of mutilated chickens and barn cats. The wolf had appeared to be on a general westward trajectory and never in one spot too long, but now it seemed to have hunkered down in Cutler County, and more specifically, somewhere in the hills along the Crow River.

Lucy believed the wolf could actually be somewhere on the Sawbrook family property, but she had yet to spot any tracks or spoor and couldn't narrow down its location much beyond their 600-acre sprawl of natural woodlands between the river and Lake Michigan.

Michigan's Department of Resources—the MDR—had yet to say anything on the record about the possibility of a gray in the northern Lower, but rumors were swirling. Farmers were concerned about livestock, and community members were on edge because they were irrationally afraid of the animal, but also because they understood, quite rationally, that laws surrounding the gray—an endangered species—came with a real cost attached. Cutler was a resort economy and federal regulations would derail development projects, cost hundreds of jobs, and hurt tourism across the board.

Lucy had tried to win some hearts and minds. She was the head ranger at Crooked Tree Park and had always believed that education and awareness were critical components of the MDR's purpose. She'd updated the park website with a page attempting to educate readers on the gray wolf and to generally demystify the supposed threat. They were pack animals, loyal to a fault, and Lucy suggested that anybody reading the article was more likely to win the lottery and be struck by a bolt of lightning on the very same day than to suffer any physical harm at the hands of a gray wolf.

She had posted the link on the park's public Facebook account, but the only thing she saw in the comments were links to dubious reports of wolf attacks or criticisms of her writing style, which people said was purposefully wordy and condescending in tone.

She'd also been booed off the mic during the town hall at the VFW for having the nerve to suggest that maybe, just possibly, everybody was overreacting to the presence of a wolf that nobody had yet confirmed.

She arrived at Victory Lanes just after ten that morning, and Ralph already had a pitcher of beer on the table. He stood up as she walked over and demanded she take her hat off.

"Why?"

"Because it says RANGER across the top in big, white letters and I told you this was on the down-low."

"How paranoid are you, Ralph?"

"Just take the hat off, Lucy. You might as well have walked in here with a neon sign."

She removed the hat, then pulled off her shades, too, but only so Ralph would be sure to see when she rolled her eyes.

"We going to have code names, too? Are you going to want to frisk me for a wire? 'Cause that's where I draw the line."

Ralph sat back down and pointed to Lucy's chair, like she couldn't do the math on where she was supposed to sit.

"I'm trying to be smart about this."

"About what?"

"You know what."

"I don't know what exactly, but it's got to be something serious to have you drag me two hours from home to watch you get drunk before lunch. My brother's an alcoholic, sober now, thank God, but he always said that if you start drinking before *The*

Price Is Right comes on, that's when it gets to be a real problem. Can they even serve this early?"

Ralph nodded toward the concession counter.

"Tommy's a friend of mine."

Tommy, the manager, and a pair of older couples bowling on the far lane were the only other people in the place, which was exactly why Ralph had chosen it. Lucy eyed the pitcher and decided to pour herself a glass. She'd gotten up early enough that it at least felt like lunch.

"Okay, Ralph. I'm here and my hat's off. What's going on?"

"Shit, what isn't going on? I got five balls in the air and I can't say which one is worse than any other because it's all so bad. I got a reporter from the *National Geographic* that called the department asking questions about a goddamn wolf that we've yet to acknowledge exists. I got the bosses in Lansing so far up my ass I can't walk straight and I got a congressman threatening to cut funding if we hit a ninety-day stop on this."

The 90-day stop was a mandatory construction freeze the federal government would impose on all "wolf-affected areas" if the gray became official. Lucy had already seen posts on social media about the horrors of a 90-day stop and how they'd all end up in soup lines if they let the government tell a developer they had to wait a few months to build another set of condominiums. People were already talking about protesting the MDR, which was pointless because the MDR could not issue a 90-day stop or even officially acknowledge the wolf existed. The Wolf Advisory Council directed all state policy on the wolf, and they had yet to even convene a meeting on the matter.

Lucy took a drink of her beer.

"Of course, we should want the stoppage. We should be begging for it, but you and the rest of the Lansing bosses are too chickenshit."

Ralph was a tall, skinny man with his head shaved bald and he wore thick, amber-framed glasses. He also wore his facial hair in a soul patch that he claimed his wife found attractive. He leaned back in his chair with his beer cupped to his chest.

"You can play high and mighty if you want, but it's your job we're trying to save. Your damn park. We got real pressure from Lansing right now, and if the MDR shuts down an entire economy over one gray? That's construction jobs and it's tourism and it's the big bad state government fucking everything up for everybody. So it can't happen. It absolutely cannot. We're already underfunded and nobody in this department is looking to take any arrows over this. I mean, if this were to happen, then you're looking at massive layoffs as retribution. They'll restructure the entire department, if they keep us around at all."

"But it's not even our call. It's the council's call."

"Council isn't touching this."

"So, what's the problem then?"

"Media. If they get ahold of it, then the council has to do something, but we get blamed because the council has been infiltrated by ringers that are doing everything they can to ignore this and run interference."

"How did it get to be that a Wolf Advisory Council is running interference for a bunch of politicians and developers?"

"Is that a real question?"

"Yes. I thought they were supposed to be the good guys."

"Two seats are reserved for academics and scientists. Two

seats are appointed by Congress. One seat is elected by the tribe."

"So, that should be three to two in favor of the good guys."

"The bad guys slipped a ringer into the academic seat. That seat is appointed by a committee and they stacked the committee by holding a midnight vote to change the way the committee is appointed. Is that enough layers of bureaucracy for you?"

Lucy got into public service to work outdoors and protect the natural world but it always seemed to come down to some nameless schlub on some obscure committee, and the people that paid attention to those arcane mechanisms and levers of power were by nature the worst sort of people and they always won because they had nothing better to do than exploit well-meaning systems for their own personal gain.

She closed her eyes and rubbed at her temples.

"Can we get to the part where you tell me what you want me to do? Why you called this weird meeting?"

"I want you to get the wolf."

"What do you mean, get it?"

"I want you to rubber-trap it and ship it back to the preserve and do it without the media catching wind. I want it to be like this wolf was never here in the first place. No construction stop, no federal government, no red tape. No goddamn *National Geographic*. That's the plan."

"You ever think about how the whole point of that program was to reintroduce these animals into the wild, and now that they've done it, we want to act like it didn't happen because some limp-dick congressman thinks it will be bad for the economy?"

"We don't *think* it will be bad for the economy, we fucking know it, Lucy. Which isn't to mention, I'm trying to save the wolf here, too. Let's not get that part twisted."

"You're trying to save the wolf by snapping its leg in a rubber trap and sending it back to the UP?"

"I'm trying to save this wolf from the poachers that the developers are going to hire to come and get this thing before we do."

"So now we're letting poachers call the shots?"

"They want to kill this wolf and bury it in a field somewhere. They want to erase it entirely."

"This is not how any of this is supposed to work. I'm pretty sure this is the exact opposite of how this is supposed to work."

"Nothing works, Lucy. There's like two things in the history of the world that have actually worked the way they were supposed to, and that's why nobody knows what the fuck to do with this wolf. We weren't prepared for the possibility. Oh, and the sheriff's department is no good on this. *Your* sheriff's department. Up in Cutler."

"What does that mean?"

"It means they're looking the other way. Developers don't want anybody on the law side messing with this poacher, and they got Sheriff Dunn to play along."

"So there's a specific poacher? This isn't just in the abstract?"

"I don't think it's in the abstract, no."

"Where did you hear all this?"

"Where didn't I? It's in the wind, Lucy. It's in the halls of Congress and in the diners and it's on the message boards. Fuck, I don't know, somebody probably scrawled it on the bathroom wall of a rest stop on Highway 75. It's what's happening."

"Do they know who?"

"Who what?"

"Who the poacher is, and who's doing the hiring?"

"I have no idea. There might even be more than one outfit hiring more than one poacher. What I'm saying is, the wheels are turning and the sheriff's department is in the loop. You see something and go to them, they're going to use it against all of us. Against the wolf, for sure. That's how bad it is. That's how much pressure we're all under with this fucking thing."

"I don't know when we became such cowards, but I hate it."

"There's some cowardice to it. I'll acknowledge it. But what are we going to do if they cut us, Lucy? This is a battle we got to let go of to stay in the war. You stay in this job long enough and you'll get to a point where you realize that being right doesn't always matter. In fact, it hardly ever does. It's just the way of the world."

"No matter what happens, Ralph, I want to be clear that to me being right is the only thing that matters. It's the only thing that ever will matter. The second I lose that, you can rubber-trap me and send me out to pasture because it is over."

"I just don't want to lose my job, Lucy. And I don't want you to lose yours."

"Stop doing that. Stop making it like it's a favor for me. At least be honest about that part."

"Fine. I do not want to lose my job two years before retirement and have to get a job at the Walmart. I do not want that to happen to me. Is that better?"

Lucy had finished her first cup of beer and poured another.

"Now who's got the problem?" said Ralph.

"I'm drinking it so you don't," she said. "I'm doing this for you."

Pins crashed in the far alley and Lucy looked over at the old couples. They were shouting and high-fiving. Her parents didn't bowl, but it still brought them to mind—the way those couples still seemed to enjoy each other—and it made her miss them both. They'd been gone nearly a year now, but the grief still cut her to the quick—like a sudden gust of cold autumn wind late in the summer.

"Can I ask you something, Ralph?"

"Shoot."

"What am I supposed to do about these poachers?"

"You're supposed to get the wolf before they do."

"And what if I don't?"

"Then help them bury it."

Lucy did not check her phone before she headed home. She never even considered it. She just gassed up and drove the two hours from West Branch with her windows down and the stereo up.

She'd bought a brand-new F-150 that spring, but only because her father had told her that everybody should buy one truck fresh off the lot in their life—that a brand-new truck was a particular pleasure and indulgence that had to be experienced to be understood. He told her that as foolish as buying brand-new was, it was worth it, just the once.

"You got to be smart about what you're foolish over," he'd told her. "Everybody is going to be a fool for something, so choose good things and you won't be as likely to fall for the bad ones."

The truck was sable blue and she went with the extended

cab and paid extra to have a stereo with a CD player put in. That one had thrown the salesman.

"Really?" he'd said. "The stock is real nice, you've got the aux port and the Bluetooth—"

"I got three hundred CDs I bought over the course of my life and I'm not getting rid of them."

"You know you can stream all those, anyway. Everything is on Spotify or whatever it is you prefer."

"I prefer my CDs and I've tried to do the Bluetooth and I don't want all that shit on my phone and I don't want to be poking at my phone all the time to try and pull something up. I like to put in a CD and listen to it for a while and then put another one in and listen to it."

The salesman relented. Held up his hands, palms out. Told her he'd see what he could do.

She paid an upcharge to go backward in technology and believed it was as good a decision as she'd ever made in her life. She didn't want access to every song in the world at every moment of every day—all those choices were goddamn exhausting—and she didn't want an algorithm explaining what she liked because she already knew, didn't need to be told.

Cat Power was playing her guitar and blowing through a harmonica and the highway before her was open in both lanes. It was bright in the early afternoon and she looked out at the flat of mid-Michigan and the soy fields beneath the irrigators. The clouds in the distance were thin above the line of the horizon, and the sky was like a blue terracotta glaze, and she pushed the gas pedal down harder.

She was not going to help any poacher bury anything and

she was not going to rubber-trap any wolf and send it back to the preserve. What she could do was leak the story to the media, maybe call this reporter from the *National Geographic* and get the 90-day stop and seize control of the narrative.

They didn't teach them about narratives at Michigan Tech, but she had started a nonprofit to protect the river and the Sawbrook acreage and learned quickly how important those were.

They were likely too late on the wolf, though. There was a reason she'd been booed at the VFW, and it wasn't like a 90-day stop would accomplish much beyond whatever frustration and short-term losses the developers and politicians sustained. Those would be victories, and satisfying to be sure, but not enough to stem the tide in a meaningful way.

Lucy knew the program in the federal preserve was working, she had heard nothing but good things, and now a strong young wolf had dispersed and set out to find territory and claim a pack of its own.

The species had clawed its way back from the brink of extinction and was on the edge of reclaiming ground they'd had taken from them over a century prior, and if she could keep the wolf free for just a little bit longer—if she could protect the animal from the poachers and her own department—some others might just follow.

A pack of grays in the wild in the northern Lower would drop the hammer on so much more than a 90-day stop. A real pack in the wild would lead to protracted congressional shit fights, sustained media attention, and maybe, just maybe, the construction and expansion could slow to the point that the gold rush ended and the developers pulled up stakes and left. It was ambitious, to be sure, but the one resource developers had never possessed was patience. And even if they didn't run off scared, never to return, it didn't change the fact that fighting to keep that wolf in the wild was the right thing to do.

She needed to locate the wolf, though. She needed to see it and put eyes on it and then she could work to establish a perimeter and turn her own property, essentially, into a preserve.

She could put up fladry to redirect the wolf away from the river and point it toward the various creeks and streams on Sawbrook land, and if she knew where the wolf was bedding she could patrol for roadkill and reduce the likelihood that it would come out of the hills to feed.

These would be difficult things to execute, but they could be done if she could pinpoint the wolf's location and reduce the family's six hundred acres to a manageable area.

The funny thing was, she had yet to see a single track. They'd twice heard howling on the property, and she'd heard rumors of a dead cat and tracks along the river, but she had yet to see anything for herself and she had looked every day for weeks. There was part of her that thought the whole thing might still be some sort of elaborate hoax—some twisted kids torturing cats and going to crazy lengths to frame a fictional wolf. She didn't think that was likely, but in this day and age you could never be completely certain.

Lucy saw Jewell standing on her front porch just as soon as she crested the hill at the end of their property road. Buckner was in the field between Jewell's house and the tree line, tossing a football with some boy Lucy had never seen in her life, and Jewell was pissed about something. She could feel the heat of her sister's anger from fifty yards away, could see it in the hard way she leaned against the porch railing, and Lucy braced herself for whatever this was going to be.

She parked right in front of Jewell's house and hadn't even stepped out of the truck before Jewell lit into her.

"Are you deliberately ignoring me, or did you turn off your notifications again?"

"I didn't deliberately do anything. Did you text me or something?"

"I texted you a hundred times. I called you like, fifty."

"About what?"

"Are you serious?"

"Yes."

"You haven't seen your phone?"

"No."

"Jesus Christ, you're worse than Mom was."

"What's the big deal? What's going on?"

"What's going on is that kid over there playing catch with Buckner."

"What about him?"

"You really don't know?"

"I'm not making this up, Jewell. I promise."

"I don't even know where to start."

"How about you start at the start?"

"That boy over there playing catch with our brother claims to be our cousin."

Lucy laughed.

"I'm serious," Jewell went on. "Second cousin, technically."

"Our cousins are all grown."

"Delos would disagree."

Lucy watched the boy track down a long pass from her brother.

"That's his name, Delos?"

"Delos Harris."

"And what's he doing here?"

"Just claiming to be our cousin and playing catch with Buckner. They're like two peas in a pod already."

"He's not our cousin, Jewell. Or second cousin or whatever. Unless one of Daddy's nieces adopted a kid, I guess—"

"It's not Daddy's side he's claiming. That's why there's a hundred messages on your phone for you to ignore. He's not a Clark. He says he's a Sawbrook."

"What?"

"I'm dead serious."

Lucy pulled the brim of her ranger hat lower, tried to shield a little more of the sun as she turned back to her sister.

"C'mon, Jewell."

"You think I'd blow your phone up over a Clark? Shit, if it was a Clark I'd be inside watching TV, not pacing the porch like a maniac."

"Is this a joke? Because it's pretty twisted and definitely not funny."

"I'm not joking! He's not, either."

"Mom's brother and sister both died young. They didn't have kids. You know that. This is some sort of sick prank."

"Tell that to his face, because the more I look at him, the more he looks like Mom."

"Oh, Jesus Christ. I don't have time for any of this. I just wanted to get some food for lunch but I can't even do that without walking into some craziness."

"He just showed up here," Jewell said. "This wasn't how I expected to spend my morning, I'll tell you that."

"What do you mean, he showed up here?"

Jewell pointed across the field to where she'd first seen the boy that morning.

"I looked up and he was standing right there. He fucking appeared out of the ether. Then we went inside and I fed him, and I saw that picture of Mom and her siblings, you know, the one on the wall in the hallway?"

"What about it?"

"I mean, she was about his age in that photo and it's fucking eerie how much they look alike."

"I'll punch you square in your face, Jewell. If this is some sort of setup, I swear to God I will fucking put your lights out."

"Go look for yourself."

"I'm going to work."

Lucy turned to walk back to her truck, and when Buckner saw her getting ready to leave, he tossed the football to the boy and ran over to head her off.

"Luce," he said. "Did you hear we got a cousin?"

"Second cousin," said Jewell.

"No cousin," said Lucy. "Both our aunt and uncle died young. There is no cousin or even the possibility of one."

"He's a fucking Sawbrook if I've ever seen one," said Buckner. "He looks just like Mom in that picture. Did Jewell tell you?"

"I told her. She didn't want to listen."

Buckner went on.

"Plus, he's quick and he's got great hands. You see that one he just tracked down? I'm telling you, this kid has some real talent."

"You've known him for two hours," said Jewell.

"When you know, you know. That's a fucking Sawbrook as sure as I'm standing here."

Lucy retook her stride toward the truck.

"I can't deal with any of this."

"We need your help," said Buckner. "Please, Lucy."

"No, you don't."

"We kind of do," said Jewell.

Lucy climbed into the driver's seat and turned the key in the ignition, but her window was still down and now Buckner was shouting through it.

"He says he knows where the wolf is!"

Lucy flinched at the nearness of her brother, at the sheer size of him and the way he filled the window frame—brow all sweaty and eyes all twitchy and excited.

"Would you back your big head up out of my cab. Jesus, God, Buckner, I swear your head gets a little bigger every day. Dripping fucking sweat droplets all over my upholstery, good Lord."

Buckner took a step back. Patted the top of his head with both hands.

"It's not getting bigger," he said. "It only looks that way because I just cut my hair."

"I have to go, Buckner. Seriously."

"He said he's seen the wolf three times."

"Okay, this keeps getting better and better. Not only is that kid our cousin, but he's the only person in the county that's actually seen the wolf, and he's seen it not once, not twice, but three times."

Lucy shifted into reverse but kept her foot on the brake.

Buckner reached out and held the driver's door through the open window.

"Luce, you need to hear him out. I promise you that you'll be glad you did. If I'm wrong, I'll get your truck detailed and fill it up with gas."

"You should do that anyway, for sweating all over my shit."

"Seriously," he said. "Shut off the truck and come inside and let's sit down. You're going to want to hear this."

delos

There were things I said that morning to the Sawbrooks, and other things I didn't. I did say that I had run away from foster care, but I sort of made it seem like I'd left the county facility rather than the Bakers' house, and I damn sure didn't mention any stolen rifles. I didn't lie about the wolf, though. I told the Sawbrooks everything I knew about that. Well, not exactly everything right off.

Lucy had a pen and a notebook and was writing down some of the stuff I said, and when she asked me if I could draw her a map and point out where I'd seen the tracks along the river I told her that I could.

I'm good at sketching things and I think that might have saved me right off. I think Buckner and Jewell mostly believed what I was telling them, maybe Buckner a little bit more than Jewell, but I don't think Lucy was buying anything I sold until I drew that little map of the river and showed her exactly where I'd seen the tracks. Then I told her I'd been covering them up, too.

"Why would you do that?"

"Because I didn't want the wrong person finding them."

"Smart," said Buckner. "That was really smart, dude."

"Anyway," Lucy said. "What can you tell me about where those tracks went?"

"I can tell you exactly where they went, but I need something in return."

I could tell that pissed Lucy off. She leaned back in her chair and stared me straight in the eyes.

"You're trying to cut a deal?"

"Yes, ma'am."

"Proof he's a Sawbrook," said Buckner.

"Proof he's got an angle," said Lucy.

They talked to each other like I wasn't even there, but I understood why Lucy was upset. We were all supposed to be on the same side when it came to the wolf, so I shouldn't be cutting deals over that, but I only had one piece of information that was of any value at all and I couldn't afford to just give it away.

Lucy cut right to the chase.

"What do you want?"

"I don't want to go back to county. I hate it there, and it's beautiful here on this property."

Lucy looked at both Buckner and Jewell now. Lucy was irritated but Buckner and Jewell looked a little bit like they were having fun, which I think made Lucy even angrier.

"You told me what you don't want. What's the deal here, specifically?"

"I'd like to stay on the property tonight. If I can do that, I'll tell you where to go to find the wolf."

"You telling me where to go doesn't do me any good unless I find the wolf. So, if the wolf is where you say it is, then you can stay the night on the property. One night. But no wolf, no stay."

"Deal."

I stuck my hand out, shook with Lucy, then she told me to shake with Buckner and Jewell as well.

"You cut a deal with one of us, it's with all three. Understood?"

"Yes, ma'am."

Buckner clapped.

"Let's go fishing, dude," he said. "I'll show you where we catch trout."

lucy

Lucy found the boy's claims about multiple wolf sightings dubious, particularly that he had seen the wolf both in Woodyard and in Cutler, and was close to dismissing his story entirely until he brought up the one spot on the river she had always believed that a wolf would most likely come to for water. The boy drew his map, then she cut the deal, told him to draw the rest of it, and went to pack her rucksack for the hike.

One thing Lucy couldn't figure about the wolf was why it would be strolling the woods along Cut Road. There should be plenty to eat on the other side of the river, but if the boy was to be believed about the sightings, then there was clearly a pattern of movement that had been established on both sides of the Crow.

As far as his claims of bloodline went, they were utterly preposterous, except for the undeniable fact that he looked so much like their mother that she found it deeply unnerving.

Buckner and the boy had already decamped and Jewell was headed for a nap when Lucy set out. She'd thought at least one of her siblings would pester her to come along, which would have been a terrible idea, and she was glad to have avoided that particular argument as she rode a four-wheeler into the forest behind their houses.

Off river, the Sawbrook land was dense with pine and birch. The forest stretched in every direction and was only interrupted, on occasion, by a creek, shallow ravine, or large outcropping of sandstone.

Lucy did not go to the Crow, but drove the ATV directly to where the boy had said the tracks led—a big rock about a quarter mile up the first slope that rose from the river. Lucy could see trampled brush in the woods where the wolf might have come and gone, and above her, in the distance, was the first ridge of outcroppings where she believed the wolf could realistically be bedding.

She left the four-wheeler there and the hike turned steep quickly as it angled up through the rutted forest and big, smooth stretches of stone where she could see the wide expanse of pines and the sun above the hills, bathing the rock ledge in shadow.

The sky was high and wide and clear of clouds and she thought of her parents as she climbed. She felt their presence in the pine boughs and in the fine, dusty gravel on the rock face and in the cool air off the river. She felt all the generations that came before, too, and before the Sawbrooks it had been the Odawa and their own generations and legacies and lineage, and their dreams had been just as tender and true as her own. In the end that had not mattered nearly as much as it should have.

She could not reclaim the Odawa's dreams or make them her own, but she was not haunted by them, either. Not any more than she was haunted by her own people. The Sawbrook dead did not speak, or whisper their counsel in the wind, and neither did the Odawa, and it would have been an insult to all of them to think otherwise. They had said their words when they were on the land in the flesh and they had died for that acreage, and their lives had been redeemed in their death because they had emptied themselves and left nothing behind but stories and bone. On the property the dead became the piney earth and the damp rock, and that was all they would ever be and all she would ever be, and it was the only thing she had ever truly wanted.

This was why the wolf had returned over a hundred years later, because this place that had once been good enough for its own packs to thrive was still there and it was still bountiful with rabbit and squirrel and water, and if they did not protect that wolf with everything they had, then they were a failure to the land and deserved it even less than they already did.

Lucy only stopped her climb once, to drink from her canteen, and the water was cold and bitten with a hard, mineral tang, and when she wiped the edges of her mouth with a shirt-sleeve she saw scat just beneath her and knew that she was very close.

She moved along the rock in a crouch until she saw mud prints around a narrow opening in the rock face and she took off her rucksack, unzipped the front pocket, and pulled out a raw steak.

This was poor form, to offer the wolf this piece of meat, but she allowed herself to do it just the once, just to see the animal and draw it near this first time.

The meat was bundled in butcher paper and she removed it from the wrapper and tossed the slab a few feet in front of her on the rock shelf.

She did not have to wait long. The cave was dark but she saw a flicker of light across the wolf's eyes and her heart seized up and sat like a brick in the center of her chest.

The animal came forward, slowly, and she could hear its nails clack against the stone and its body filled the cave and scraped the walls with its coarse fur, and when it emerged to claim the food its head was massive and hard-lined—all jaw and broad snout.

They were so close she could feel the heat of the wolf's breath when its jaw dropped open to let its tongue loll. She could see the black, gummy flaps that edged his mouth and his long teeth and how sharp they were. His ears were towering and perfectly straight and his nose was damp and the edges of his nostrils were flared.

She stared at him and the wolf stared back at her. Its eyes were black and rimmed with pale-blue arcs and she did not turn away. She could not turn away. She was frozen and she stared until the wolf let out a sigh and dipped its massive head to gather the meat slab and disappeared back inside the stone.

Lucy remained crouched. For a moment, she could not move. She may not have even breathed. She could hear the lapping of the wolf's big, wet tongue and its teeth snapping like snare drums as it tore through the steak.

part II

darnette

Darnette Lewis had served twenty-eight days of a thirty-day bid in the county jail for violation of probation, and was getting out one day early for good time.

The night before his release he was pulled out of his cell and taken into the front of the jail and placed in the holding tank.

Nobody told him what was happening, of course. They just ripped him out of his usual nightly routine, which would have been a welcome break from the monotony any other time, but now that he was on the eve of his release it did nothing but worry him.

He'd pissed dirty on a random test, that was his violation, and he did a quick catalog of the weeks preceding that slipup in case there was anything he'd done that might have come back to bite him while he was cooped up on the inside. He couldn't think of anything offhand, but that didn't absolve him.

He'd been drinking a fair amount that June and there were some blank spots here and there where he could have been committing any number of felonies or heinous acts for which he was about to pay the price.

There comes a time when you've crossed the law enough that you can never be certain you are truly free. Darnette had accepted long ago that every wail of every siren he ever heard would produce in him a quick but sharp flash of anxiety and dread, and that was just the cost of doing business outside the narrow parameters of the law. So he sat in the empty holding tank and he stewed and felt his stomach roil as he waited and then Sheriff Dunn came walking into the room outside of the cell.

"There he is," said Darnette. "The Grand Pooh-Bah himself."

Sheriff Dunn did not acknowledge Darnette. He was reading something on his phone and made his slow way forward.

Darnette had never seen a man waddle like the sheriff. Dunn was a big man, and he probably logged more miles going side to side than he did moving forward. One step forward, two steps sideways, that was Sheriff Edward Dunn's way of moving through the world.

Dunn arrived at the cell and finally looked up from his phone.

"Darnette, mind if I come in and have a sit?"

The sheriff put the key card against the lock and the light flipped green and the door made its heavy buzzing sound and slid open.

Dunn eased himself down on the bench at the opposite end from Darnette. The sheriff was about busting at the seams in his uniform and there was sweat glistening on his forehead and big blooms of old stains underneath his arms. He took a hanky from his pocket and mopped at his face.

"Hot out there tonight?"

"Muggy," said Dunn.

Darnette cleared his throat and straightened his seated posture.

"I haven't done a goddamn thing, Sheriff. I promise you that whatever you heard is nothing but baseless lies and slander."

"How do you know what I hear?"

"I don't. I'm just saying that if you're here because somebody has taken up lies against my character, then I need to let you know right off that I have been walking the straight and narrow. I'm not even glancing off the path of righteousness, Sheriff. Not these days."

"I'm not here to arrest you."

"Okay. So a social call then? That's flattering. I wasn't expecting a drop-in from a high-ranking official such as yourself, but let's lean into it. Let's chop it up a little bit."

"This isn't social, either."

"So, you didn't come to shoot the shit or inquire about my life and its many interesting developments in the time since we last spoke?"

"Have there been some developments, Darnette?"

"I've come to feel differently about some things. I have gone through some changes that have been interesting to me. Different philosophies have emerged in my thinking."

"Well, I don't give a shit about any of that, obviously."

"And yet I consider it an honor to speak with a man of your esteem. I don't mind saying so, either."

"Jesus Christ, Darnette. I forgot about this part."

"About what part?"

"The way you talk."

"How do I talk?"

"Too much."

"Well, you're not giving me much to work with."

"I came here with an opportunity, Darnette. Don't make me regret it."

"What kind of opportunity?"

"There's a man waiting to speak with you. He'll come in as soon as I leave. Whatever happens after that is up to you."

"What man? Do I know him?"

"No, you do not."

"What's his name?"

"People call him Davenport."

"Is that his name?"

"That's what he's called."

"What the fuck is this?"

"Like I said, it's an opportunity."

Sheriff Dunn stood up and walked his slow way out of the cell and back across the room. Then the far door buzzed open and a man walked in as Dunn walked out.

This man was wearing a polo top, slacks, and boat shoes. He had on a baseball hat with no logo or insignia and wore a pair of dark sunglasses with silver frames.

This man walked with a fast, purposeful stride—a regular bolt of lightning compared to Sheriff Dunn. He was short, but his arms bulged with muscle and Darnette recognized him immediately as a former lawman or military type. Maybe both. Probably both.

"Davenport, I presume," said Darnette.

The man sat down on the bench. He sat much closer than Dunn had and smelled sharply of cologne.

"Davenport, or some people call me Port. Either one."

"Well, don't I feel like the belle of the ball? All this attention on my last night inside. What can I help you with?"

"I hear you're a hunter."

"Shit, Port, I'm the best hunter I've ever met."

"Great. I've got the right guy, then."

"The right guy for what?"

"There's going to be an envelope at your house when you return home tomorrow. Inside that envelope is some cash to get you outfitted with whatever supplies you need. All that has to be on the down-low, though. Don't buy this shit online or at the fucking Cabela's. You follow me?"

"I heard something about cash. I'm following that part."

"You can keep the equipment when you're done. Whatever you buy will be yours. This first installment of cash is fifteen hundred. We figure seven fifty to get you ready, another seven fifty as a show of good faith. Additionally, you'll receive one payment of ten thousand dollars when the task is complete."

"What am I getting outfitted for?"

"The removal of a gray wolf."

"A gray wolf?"

Davenport nodded.

"We're fairly certain there's one loose in the county somewhere, but you need to be quick about it and discreet. Very quick. Very discreet. And the wolf needs to be gone, gone."

"Gone how?"

"Treat it like you would a dead body and up and disappear it.

I don't care how, but it has to be removed entirely from the face of the earth. Nobody can know you killed it, or that it was here in the first place."

"I'm not sure exactly what you're saying, being that I have never worked with dead bodies in any way, shape, or form."

"It's not that complicated, Darnette. I would suggest just burying it. Nobody's going to come looking for it or dig it up. Once it's gone, it's gone."

"Gray wolves are an endangered species, Port."

"Hence the ten K."

"What if I say no?"

"Then I leave and you don't get paid and I never talk to you again. But if you accept, and then try to fuck us and take off with our money, or run your mouth about any of this, I'll cut off two fingers."

"Jesus, man. Calm down. I'm not trying to steal anybody's money here. You offered me this gig."

"That's the deal. You can take it or leave it."

"What's the sheriff's role in all this?"

"To stay out of your way. You don't have to worry about the law on this, Mr. Lewis. You just have to worry about the wolf."

"I'll do it."

"Excellent. Sounds like we've got a deal, then."

Darnette stuck out his hand, but Davenport did not shake it. Davenport just stood up and walked out of the cell. He didn't seem like a man that liked to bother with pleasantries, so Darnette tried not to take it too personally, but he did. If only just a little.

the sawbrooks

Out at the Sawbrook property, the siblings and Buckner's wife, Sky, were gathered around a bonfire. Jewell had made pork chops and applesauce for dinner, and then they'd let the boy roast some marshmallows before he went to sleep at Jewell's.

Frog, Sky and Buckner's toddler, was conked out in the trailer and Buckner had brought out the monitor and set it beside his lawn chair. The speaker made its quiet, staticky sound while the fire lapped at the pallet that Lucy had thrown down earlier to burn. She'd already told them about the wolf, and she and Delos had compared notes on their sightings.

"It's big," she had said. "It's a healthy, young, male gray and it came down here to start a pack of its own."

Delos asked if that meant it was an alpha, which allowed her to explain that while it probably would become an alpha were it to find a mate and breed, it wasn't an alpha in the sense that he might be thinking. An alpha gray wolf was not about dominance so much as it was about leadership, decision-making, and caring for the pack.

"See," Buckner said to the boy. "Look at all this cool shit you can learn around here."

The boy pulled a marshmallow off the top of his stick and smiled.

"Yes, sir."

Jewell walked him up to the house for bed just before dark, and when she returned she brought beer for her sister and Sky, and a cold root beer for Buckner.

They all cracked their drinks and got down to discussing the boy. Buckner was convinced he was blood, Jewell was nearly certain, and Lucy said it didn't matter what she thought because they were going to figure it out with some DNA kits and good old-fashioned research.

"He's not telling us something," Jewell said. "That much I do know."

"Did he say anything just now?" Buckner asked. "When you took him up to the house?"

"He didn't. But it's more how quiet he is."

"There's probably more than one thing he's not telling us," said Lucy. "If I had to guess."

Jewell agreed, but Buckner wasn't sure. He was a little surprised by Jewell's position on the matter, too.

"Why do you say that, Jewell?"

"Because of how he showed up out of the blue, just standing in the field looking like *Children of the Corn*. He had to come here running from something."

"He said he was in foster care. That's probably reason enough to run."

There was a bit of wind from the hills and Jewell tilted to the side as smoke funneled in her direction from the fire.

"We can't just keep him here, Buckner. You know that."

"Well, I'm worried we're putting him back in a harmful situation. You know terrible things happen in those places."

Sky had been looking at something on her phone, and now she glanced up.

"Mary Miller is still working at the county foster facility. She's as good as gold. We can take him to her. She won't put a child into harm's way."

Jewell raised an eyebrow.

"Mary Miller still works there?"

Sky lifted her phone.

"I just searched it. There's a picture of her on their Instagram account from yesterday."

"That's a great idea, Sky," said Lucy. "That's exactly what we'll do."

Buckner smiled at his wife, then turned to his sisters.

"She just always knows the move. It's crazy."

"I mean, other than marrying you, I agree," said Jewell.

"Everybody's got their blind spots," said Buckner.

"I've got wolf stuff to do in the morning," said Lucy. "Can you guys handle taking Delos?"

"We'll take him," said Jewell. "Me and Buck."

"We're all on the same page, right?" Buckner asked. "If this boy is a Sawbrook we're getting custody and bringing him back here to the property to live? We'll get a lawyer if we have to. That's where I stand on it."

"Of course," said Jewell.

"If the DNA comes back with a match, then absolutely," Lucy said. "No questions asked."

"What about the wolf?" Sky said. "What's the plan there?"

"The MDR wants me to rubber-trap it and get it back up to the national forest. Wants me to do it on the down-low without the media finding out."

"Let me guess," said Sky. "So they don't get the ninety-day stop?"

Lucy took a drink of her beer.

"Exactly."

Jewell turned to her sister.

"You guys are supposed to protect the wolf."

"I didn't say I was doing it. I said that's what they wanted me to do."

"Are you going to leak it to the media, then?"

"I thought about that, but then I thought we could do better. Maybe we can keep it here on the property. It came down here to start a pack and stake out its own territory. It came further south than I would have guessed, but it's here for a reason and I want to try and keep it safe until some others follow him down."

"Will they do that?" asked Sky.

"They might, yeah."

Buckner lifted up his cap and ran his fingers over his short bristles of hair.

"So you just want to hide him up here?"

Lucy shrugged.

"Why not?"

"No reason," he said. "Except how do you even do that?"

"There's things we can do. It's a lot of time and effort, and it might not work, but there are ways we can increase the odds. The first thing is to keep it off the river. We need to make some fladry and string it up."

"What the fuck is fladry?" asked Buckner.

"It's basically just red flags on a rope that will keep the wolf from crossing under it. You redirect it from the river and push it in toward the middle of the property so it can drink out of the creeks and the streams. It's not something we can order without looking real suspicious, but we could make it. Buckner and Jewell, you're both pretty good with a sewing machine."

"How long of a rope?" asked Jewell.

"Pretty fucking long," said Lucy. "Like I said, it'll be a chore."

"What else needs to be done?" said Sky.

Here, Lucy paused. Stared at the fire and considered what she was about to say. The flames were higher now, and hot. She took a drink of cold beer and then leaned backward in her lawn chair.

"I couldn't figure out why the wolf would be over there by Cut Road. I didn't believe the kid at first, but then I saw the markings tonight and there's definitely a route he's taking to cross.

"But then I wondered, Why? There's plenty to eat and drink on this side of the river, but the one thing we don't have as much of is roadkill. That's what Cut Road is known for, right? Fucking roadkill. And for a wolf hunting on its own, that's a pretty big payday. So, we can keep the wolf off the other side of the river with the fladry, but we're going to need to keep our roads on this side clear, too. That way he doesn't come down and get seen picking at a dead deer or something."

"What's that have to do with Sky?" said Buckner.

"I was thinking she and Frog could take a lap, once or twice a day, just get out on these river roads and look for any carcasses. And if they find any, get them disposed of in a hurry."

Sky turned to Buckner.

"Oh God, he's going to love that. He loves a car ride."

"Educational, too," said Buckner.

"Done," said Sky. "We're on it."

"I feel like you got the fun job," said Buckner.

"I can't sew," she said. "You're a victim of your own expertise."

Jewell tipped her beer in Lucy's direction.

"What are you going to do? Just sit up in your ivory tower and devise strategies?"

"No," said Lucy. "I'm going to deal with the poachers."

delos

Morning came sooner than I expected. Maybe it was all that fresh air on the property, but I felt like the second I closed my eyes, they snapped back open. It wasn't even sunrise yet. There was gray light out the window and I had no idea why I'd woken up until I saw Buckner standing outside telling me to get ready.

"Get up, dude."

"For what?"

I sat up in bed and Buckner poked his big head through the window.

"Just hurry up," he whispered. "Come right out the window here and be quiet about it. Meet me at the porch."

I tossed my blanket off, crawled out the window, and stepped outside in my bare feet. The air was cold and the grass was dewy wet and it sounded like there were a million birds in the pines. I could still see stars above the trees as I walked around the front of the house and found Buckner waiting. He was sitting on the front steps holding two cups of coffee and he handed me a mug.

I don't drink coffee, but I took it because I was cold and it was steaming warm and that mug was hot against the inside of my palm and warmed me.

"I didn't give you any cream or sugar."

I looked down at the cup.

"That's okay. I don't really drink coffee, anyway."

"How old are you?"

"Fourteen."

"Yeah, you should probably get started. Coffee is good for you and I started you on the black—that way you don't get to where you need cream and sugar. None of us Sawbrooks uses either and were never offered any by our parents. You start drinking it black, that way it's what you're used to and then you save the money and the hassle of needing extras."

"I guess that makes sense."

"It makes perfect sense, but don't drink any yet. It's hot as shit and you'll burn your tongue."

Buckner stood up and began to walk toward where he and his siblings parked their vehicles, and I followed. I didn't ask where we were going, but we climbed in one of the pickups, the older one, and took it off property and then turned upriver.

I thought he was going to take me fishing. We hadn't caught anything the day before, which had irked him, and I thought maybe we were going to try and hook some trout for breakfast or something cool like that, but instead he took me all the way up to the falls before he parked the pickup and killed the engine.

"Go on and drink that coffee now," he said. "You'll want the warmth here in a minute."

That coffee tasted like hot dirt and I nearly spit it all over Buckner's dashboard. I kept it in, though, then swallowed it and almost shivered right out of my spine. I felt my nasal passages open up and I was all of the sudden wide-awake—from the coffee and from the wind off the river when I got out of the truck and followed Buckner toward the falls.

"What are we doing?"

"We're not doing anything," he said. "You're about to take the river falls and I'm going to stand here with my coffee and watch."

The falls separated the swampy end of the river from the resort and it was about a twenty-foot drop from a single rock ledge into still, deep water below. Buckner was telling me something, but I couldn't hear him above the sound of the falling water. I hoped he was saying that he was only kidding about me riding the falls, and I was fairly certain he was. I'd heard he was crazy, but throwing me over a waterfall before sunup seemed a little too out of pocket, or at least that's what I told myself.

He pointed at something in the river and began to head up the bank. I followed behind him and when I asked him if he was serious, he stopped walking and whipped around.

"About what?"

"I don't know. All of it. The falls and whatnot."

"Shit, yes, I'm serious. This is how you become an adult in the Sawbrook family. It's a rite of passage. I did it the first time when I was twelve. My sisters did it when they were more your age, like thirteen or fourteen."

"So you want me to go over those falls right now?"

"How many times do you need me to say it?"

"How, though?"

I was hoping he would say there was a big, inflatable raft, or a harness of some sort, but he didn't.

"You just get out into the middle of the river and let the current take you over. There's nothing to it, honestly. The only way you can really fuck it up is if you get afraid and start flailing around. If you come off it sideways you can get hurt, but as long as you just let it carry you it's no biggie. It's fun is what it is."

"So just let it take me over?"

"Yup. And don't be afraid."

Buckner went back to walking upstream and I went back to following and we were probably fifty yards from the drop when he finally sat down on a log just off the bank.

"Drink some more coffee," he said. "You'll be glad you did when you get in that river."

I didn't shiver this time, but I turned away from Buckner so I could wince pretty good.

"Jewell and Lucy are going to do some research. DNA. I don't know what else. It's Lucy's idea, mainly. She went to college and is scientific in her thinking, and she got Jewell to go along with it. They ordered some tests off the internet and Lucy did some Google searching and found some information, but who knows what that all adds up to?

"I already know you're a Sawbrook because you're a spitting image, plus you're fast and can catch a football, and you knew where the wolf was. I don't need any more proof than that, except for this river falls right here. You take this falls right now, then we'll get you warmed up in the car and drive right back up the hill for breakfast and you and me will be good as gold. We'll be locked in. Understood?"

"Yes, sir."

"And that's the other thing. After you take this drop, stop fucking calling me sir."

You might think it's crazy, to throw yourself into a current and off a waterfall when you can't even swim, but I'd never wanted anything as bad as I wanted to be a Sawbrook. And I'd already made a bigger jump, the night before.

I didn't go to bed right away, when everybody else was still at the bonfire. I had some things to sort through first.

The Sawbrooks didn't know I'd stolen a rifle and had no idea that I'd get shipped back to Woodyard the second they dropped me at the Bakers', but that was exactly what would happen. I could confess to the Sawbrooks, but then they'd be knowingly harboring a fugitive, which didn't seem like something Lucy would sign up for.

My other option was to run.

I didn't want to run, but if I did, it was only logical to wonder if Jewell might have something around the house that I could borrow to help get me started.

I didn't want to steal from my cousin, but I also didn't want to take off into the wilderness with nothing but the clothes on my back and nowhere in the world to go or anybody that wanted me.

I didn't bother checking dresser drawers or underneath the mattress—Jewell was too sharp for a stash spot like that—which was something else that bothered me about that bag of coke at the Fetterings'. They must have thought I was dumb as hell to be stashing my contraband in the one place I'd never get away with hiding it. They'd made me the scapegoat and insulted my intelligence in the process.

There wasn't much in Jewell's room in the way of decorations, but there was a picture of a runner on an empty road and when I slid my hand beneath the frame I could feel a seam in the plaster where it felt like the wall had been cut.

I popped the frame off the nail, set it on the ground, and then gave the cut piece of wall a little tap and just like that I was staring inside an empty panel in the plaster where there were three rolls of cash money and a pistol.

The outside of the rolls were twenties, but I figured the numbers got bigger toward the middle, and the pistol was a .22.

I sat down on the end of the bed and thought about it for a good, long while. I could take that cash and that gun and buy a bus ticket clear to Detroit if I wanted. Maybe even further. Kids ran away every day with a lot less than what was right there in front of me, and it was damn sure better than Woodyard.

I didn't want to steal from Jewell, though. I'd finally met the Sawbrooks after all that time and I was going to rob them after they'd fed me dinner and let me roast some marshmallows? Plus, I didn't want to leave the wolf behind, and what the hell was I going to do in Detroit, anyway?

I wasn't going back to Woodyard, but I would wait until the last possible moment to run if that was the call I had to make. I was going to give the Sawbrooks every possible opportunity to change their minds, and that's how I wound up in the river—because it was not yet time to run.

I didn't stand there poking my toe in the water all hesitant, either. I knew I was going to get in and didn't see the logic in putting it off. Buckner told me it was time, so I went. I got in that river and lost the breath in my lungs from the shock of the cold.

My ankles went numb and the rocks were sharp and jagged against the pads of my feet and I stumbled forward as the river rose quickly to the hem of my shorts and it felt like being dipped in pure ice.

I took two more steps and the cold was in my blood now and felt like a pressure building—a pipe about to burst—and I dove in so I could scream underwater and not out there in the open where Buckner could hear me.

The river was dark and cloudy with mud and silt and it tasted like brine and dirt. It was like the coffee I didn't finish, but cold. I tried to touch the bottom but it wasn't there and I took on some water and coughed, and that was when I started to panic.

I reached out for branches or for anything to grab to slow my momentum and if I could have pulled myself clean out of the water at that moment I might have done it—that's how afraid I was inside that current.

The problem was, I was in the middle of the river and I could already hear the falls nearing. The drop sounded like bombs blasting and when I felt a smooth stone beneath me I thought I had a final chance at escape. I thought I had more time.

I stood on one leg and leapt, trying to get out of the current, but I had already reached the drop and the only thing my jump did was increase the height of the fall.

I believed I would die. I truly did. I was so high, I could see the tops of the pine trees and I could hear Buckner shouting from the bank as my legs bicycled the air beneath me and I finally let myself scream and I swear I was airborne so long that I heard my own screams come back in echoes off the hills. I didn't think I would ever come down.

But I did. I dropped fast and hard and when I hit the water I heard a thundercrack and then watched the world disappear into a line of pure, white brightness.

I don't think I got knocked out to where I couldn't move, but I damn sure lost consciousness because I can't remember anything between hitting the water and sitting on the side of the river with a towel draped over my shoulders and Buckner smiling and talking about my jump.

"I've never seen anything like it," he said. "You didn't take the falls, you fucking jumped over them. Don't ever do it again, because you almost overshot the deep water and hit the rocks, which would have been an issue, but that was totally badass. It was legendary, dude."

I smiled when he said that. I couldn't have stopped myself from smiling if I tried. He gave me a little shove on the shoulders and asked if I was ready to go eat and I said that I was.

For a minute, I was so happy that I thought the Sawbrooks might change their minds and keep me. I thought that somehow everything was going to be okay.

lucy

Lucy left the property just after sunrise that morning. Didn't even notice Buckner and the boy were gone. She just brewed a pot of coffee, poured it into the thermos, and took a piece of toast for the road.

There was only one spot in northern Michigan to go for affordable firearms on the quick and down-low, and that was Kendra Simmons's place out in Porcupine County. She didn't imagine many poachers in Cutler County were fitted for a wolf hunt, but didn't doubt that Kendra would have plenty of supplies for them to purchase.

Lucy graduated with Kendra, though she couldn't remember if Kendra had actually received a diploma and walked across the stage.

Kendra was a big partyer back in the day. She smoked a lot of dope and slept around, not that Lucy judged—it was just a bit of a surprise when she got serious about guns and ammo after high school and made a fair amount of money with it. Kendra Simmons started out poor as dirt, but now she had a pole barn with enough munitions for every militia member, low-grade criminal, and poacher in the entire northern Lower.

She lived right beside that barn in a trailer on a dirt road in Porcupine County and there wasn't another house within two miles. The location was discreet, though word was she had cut a deal with Sheriff Dunn and didn't need to worry too much about the law anyway.

Lucy told D-Rod, her assistant at the park, that she was doing field work that day and to call her if anything came up. Field work was not a part of Lucy's actual job as the Crooked Tree Park ranger—there was no scientific research involved with her position at all—but D-Rod didn't know any better so it was the excuse she used if she ever needed a day.

Porcupine County was mostly flat and dry, a stretch of low, rocky country between hilly Cutler and the big water, and she stopped the car about a quarter mile from Kendra's in a little stand of hardwoods where there was a seasonal road cut-in.

She took her binoculars out and fixed her line of sight on the pole barn. Only car parked at Kendra's that morning was her own—a black Cadillac Eldorado with rust splatters on the hood.

Lucy rolled her window down and cut the engine. Then she took the phone she hated out of her glove compartment and called Delray Harper—a man her own mother had occasionally, and always with great reluctance, turned to for assistance in a pinch.

Delray owned the Boogie Down Barn, a strip joint that sat catty-corner across the river from Crooked Tree Park and that he insisted on calling a club. Delray made all his money off resorters—they loved blowing their cash on lappers after eighteen holes of golf—but he was also old-school Cutler and could be counted on for discretion, and occasionally help.

She thought it might be a little bit early to call, though Delray was notorious for his late nights and early mornings—he claimed to be a super sleeper, whatever that was—and he answered on the second ring and called her by name.

"Lucy Sawbrook," he said. "What in the world could this be about? Most people text these days."

"I hate texting."

"I do, too."

"Okay, so what's the problem?"

"Nothing. You called me. What's up?"

"I got a few questions."

"About what?"

"About what's going on with this supposed wolf."

"You got questions for me about the wolf?"

"I do, actually. Yes."

"Why?"

"Because you're across the river from my park, and in that location, if there is a wolf—"

"You want to know whose side I'm on, don't you? You want to know if I'm for the wolf."

"It doesn't have to be that black and white. It doesn't have to be sides, necessarily—"

"No, it's sides. And there's one or the other. You're either for the wolf or against it. No middle ground. And I know you actually agree with me on that part. And that's why you're calling. You want to know who I'm going to call if I see the wolf—you or the poacher?"

"Do you know who the poacher is?"

"I do not. I think they'll end up being more than one, though. When it's all said and done."

"Okay. So, who's your first call? The park ranger, or—"

"I'm calling you, Lucy."

"Really?"

"You sound surprised."

"I just figure you wouldn't want the disruption to your business is all."

"Shit, I love wolves. I got a tattoo of a wolf on my left shoulder, Lucy. And it's not some standing-on-a-cliff, howling-at-the-moon, county-fair airbrushed bullshit, either. It's a wolf head, with a bunch of different colors in the eyes. It's my favorite tattoo and I've got a lot of ink."

"I didn't know that, Delray. I'm glad to hear it."

"I read your article on the internet. I found it informative, if a little pious in tone."

"Okay."

"I think the wolf will be good for business. Brings out the wild in people. I was thinking I might have a wolf themed night, matter of fact. Most of the girls here are pro-wolf."

"You're kidding me."

"I wouldn't kid you. Not about that. I've got a few scaredy-cat types, but most of these women relate to the wolf, Lucy. My girls might wear a lot of makeup and glitter, but they are not indoor types in spirit. They tend to err on the side of freedom and wildness. I'd say three out of every four of my girls are for the wolf."

"I could have used you guys at the town hall."

"For what? There's no reasoning with that angry mob. You ought to know that by now."

"I got an offer for you, then."

"Okay."

"I'd like to put up some flags around your barn. Just outside the parking lot. You sort of string them up between trees, almost like at a used car lot."

"You're talking about fladry."

Lucy was stunned silent at Delray's wolf literacy. She just sat there for a moment dumbfounded before Delray went on.

"I know what the fuck fladry is. I'm not stupid, Lucy. I told you, I love wolves. Shit, I did some peyote way back in the early nineties and I had a whole vision involving wolves. It's what led to the tattoo."

"So I could put some up?"

"Hell, yes. I'll do you one better. We'll string up some fladry and then we'll have a wolf night where we do some thematic stuff. Play wolf songs. 'Hungry Like the Wolf.' 'Werewolves of London.' That sort of thing. But then we'll distribute literature, too. Educate. I'll do some edits on your article and sharpen it up a little. Maybe we'll raise some money for a wolf charity. Hell, I don't know. We'll do something, though."

"That would be amazing, Delray."

"You know what else, let's set up a little sweatshop here. I'll pay a few of the girls overtime and we'll bring in some sewing machines and get that fladry done. We'll do it tonight, right after close. Officially, I'll say it's to keep the wolf out for the customers' sake, but really we know the real reason is to protect the wolf."

"I'm afraid to ask what you want in return."

"I'm doing this for the wolf, but while we're at it, I'd love to have the club's Labor Day picnic at your park. I want the girls to be able to bring their kids and get everybody out of the Barn and into the fresh air. End the summer right. Have some quality time together, you know? Grill out. Potato sack races. That sort of thing."

"Done and done."

"Yeah?"

"Absolutely."

"We got a deal then, Lucy. And my word is good on this."

"I know it is."

"I expect yours is, too, Lucy. I never doubted your mother's."

"You don't have to doubt mine, either."

"I didn't think I would."

"There you have it," she said. "Consider the wheels in motion."

"Hey, you know what you should do, Lucy, if you want to find out about who the poacher is—"

"Go to Kendra Simmons's and stake it out?"

"Jesus Christ," he said. "That's what you're doing right now, isn't it?"

"Yeah, I'm looking at her old beat-to-shit Eldorado as we speak."

"I swear to God, you favor your mother."

"Let's not get crazy, Delray."

Lucy hung up and put the phone back in her glove box.

She feared Delray was right. She'd never known a woman more stubborn and infuriating than Rhoda Sawbrook, but since she'd been gone Lucy had found herself, more than a few times, drifting into the vacuum her mother's absence had left in ways that did, undoubtedly, bring her mother to mind.

Rhoda had gone through the world with the sole purpose of protecting her family and her land, and Lucy had fought against her mother's blind spots and excesses and she had questioned her motivations.

Rhoda despised the resort's encroachment on the river, but it was never quite for the right reasons. After a rare legal loss in which the resort was forced by the state to reroute a drainage line, Rhoda found the ruling's language too conciliatory and its fines too lenient.

The river had been spared a bit of drainage, and while it wasn't insignificant to the Crow itself, it did nothing to assuage Rhoda's anger and so she waged a brief campaign of terror against the resorters themselves. She was in her fifties that summer, a middle-aged woman with three adult children, and she spent her August shooting golfers with a paint gun. She hit three over the span of several weeks, and each time she perched in a tree at a different hole and fired on the backswing.

"I can't shoot them all, but I can fuck up a lot of swings and turn a bunch of birdies into bogies. I might have only hit three, but every golfer on that course will be thinking of me every time they hear a branch snap."

Buckner and Jewell had applauded the behavior and ingenuity—even their father had shaken his head in admiration—but it galled Lucy to the bone. Rhoda won more than her share of battles but never understood the war she was fighting was bigger than herself.

Lucy valued the land for purer reasons than her mother—because it was the land, not because she owned it—and that distinction had mattered very much to her as a young woman. It had mattered to her mother, too. Rhoda considered Lucy's values and environmentalism a hindrance, but in her death it occurred to Lucy that maybe neither of their motivations ever mattered much at all. Maybe the only thing that mattered in the end was what her mother had done.

Rhoda's death had been a loss, but there was space now for Lucy to occupy that she could not before. She wasn't becoming her mother so much as Rhoda's leaving had granted Lucy access to the parts of herself that came so directly from her mother that Rhoda's existence itself, at times, had felt invasive.

Or maybe that was all just a bunch of pseudopsychology and the truth was much simpler—the Sawbrooks needed Rhoda to be exactly what she was, and now that she was gone the siblings, in their own unique ways, were filling the void because that was what was necessary. Either way, it was exactly the sort of thing that Lucy was no longer required to think about because her mother was gone and there was simply too much that had to get done to sit around and wonder about *why* anybody did anything.

Lucy leaned back in her seat and picked up the binoculars. She watched, and she waited.

jewell

Buckner drove Rhoda's old Cutlass toward the county facility. Jewell was in the passenger seat and Delos was in the back with his head leaned up against the window.

The mood was heavy and fraught. The boy had eaten his breakfast, but had not said anything beyond the monosyllabic responses he'd offered to some rote questions that Jewell had thrown into the silence.

How do you like the eggs?

Good.

Would you like more juice?

No, thank you.

How did you sleep?

Fine.

Jewell was trying to stave off her own doubts and gathering dread about the boy's return to the county, and his visible despair was not helping. They were taking a potential Sawbrook off property and throwing him back into the teeth of the government, and looking at the boy in the backseat she could see how devastated he was. Even worse, she could see his resemblance to her mother in the wash of light through the window glass. The sharp line of his jaw and the way his eyes were set just a little wide above his nose. The broad forehead and the hard way he looked out at the world.

They had to take him back, though. You couldn't just keep a child like a stray cat. There was a process and paperwork. They owed it to the boy to give him a real chance at a fresh start. They'd only known him for twenty-four hours and it all needed to move just a little bit slower, be a little less frantic.

They were driving along the river. The fairways across the Crow were lush with Bermuda grass and there were several carts backed up behind a tee. Jewell had steadied her resolve about the task at hand, but the silence in the car was still unbearable and finally she pointed to the sign on the shoulder of the road that read, HIAWATHA TRAIL.

"That name is from the resort. Somehow they got the rights to call this road whatever they wanted. You ever read that poem in school, Delos? *Song of Hiawatha*?"

The boy shook his head.

"It was written by this Englishman named Henry Longfellow, and he wrote the whole book about an Indian legend, which he thought was the Iroquois chief Hiawatha, but really he was writing about an Ojibwa named Nanabozho, but he either didn't know the difference or didn't care enough to change it because, I don't know, he'd already called him Hiawatha and they hadn't invented erasers yet."

"I remember that from school," said Buckner.

Jewell doubted that, but went on.

"Hell, even Crooked Tree, Lucy's park, is something the French stole from the Indians and they probably got the meaning all twisted up backwards, and what does it even matter? Nobody gives a shit."

Jewell had her window down and her arm resting on the door. She gazed out at the water.

"And do you know what the worst part of that poem is? *The Song of Hiawatha*?"

Both Delos and Buckner shook their heads. She had climbed on the soapbox as a hedge against her own discomfort, but both the boy and her brother seemed genuinely curious.

"It's beautiful," she said. "I mean, it's about the prettiest thing I've ever heard. Our mom used to read it to us when we were kids and I've got lines of that damn thing that live inside me still. And I don't even like poetry. Matter of fact, I kind of hate poetry, and yet I can quote parts of that book to you chapter and verse."

Jewell began to recite the poem, almost to herself. That's how excruciating she found the alternative of silence. That's how generally worked up she was about it all.

> *"There among the ferns and mosses,*
> *There among the prairie lilies,*
> *On the Muskoday, the meadow,*
> *In the moonlight and the starlight,*
> *Fair Nokomis bore a daughter."*

She kept reciting the poem, which comforted her in the same way it had when she was a child, and before long Delos had closed his eyes. She stopped at the end of the next stanza and Buckner leaned over and whispered.

"Poor guy is wiped out."

"I feel terrible," she said. "I hate this. I really do."

"We don't have to do it."

"Yes, we really do," she said. "Did you call Mary Miller?"

"No, I thought you were going to."

"I thought you were."

"You said you would."

"No, I didn't. I hate calling people."

"That doesn't mean you shouldn't have to do it, ever."

"Lucy told me that you said that you would call her."

"I didn't even see Lucy this morning. I was at the river with the boy."

"What were you doing at the river?"

Buckner gave a half nod in Delos's direction.

"He went over the falls."

"What?"

"Unlike anybody has ever done it. I swear to God."

"Why didn't you tell me that?"

"I didn't want you and Lucy getting all in my grill."

"Why'd you do it at all?"

"Because while you two were prattling on about DNA and ancestry kits I realized we had a way to prove it right down there on the river. But it's one of those things that you all would have discouraged and forbid. So I didn't tell you. I did it and he did it and let me tell you, he passed with flying colors. I've never seen anything like it. He got to the ledge and fucking jumped."

"What do you mean, jumped?"

"I mean somehow he stood himself up in the current, planted his foot on the ledge, and sprang off that thing like a trampoline."

"Jesus Christ, he could have been really hurt."

"I did tell him that, and not to do it again. But I'll be honest, it was badass."

Hiawatha Trail formed a T where it met Cut and Henderson Roads, and just beyond the intersection there was an exit ramp for Highway 31 and Buckner stopped at the red. Gnawed at his lip while they waited.

"I hate this light."

Jewell had dug her phone out of her purse and was looking up Mary Miller's work number.

"Half the time I run it," she said.

"I always run it," said Buckner. "But I stop first to be safe."

She pointed at Delos.

"Don't run it with him in the car."

"You see me sitting here, don't you?"

"I know. I didn't mean it like that."

"How else could you mean it?"

"I was more saying it out loud than I was telling you what to do."

The light changed and Buckner took his foot off the brake, but the moment he hit the gas the back door flew open and Delos fell out of the car onto the gravel road and he rolled clear to the shoulder, where he popped up and then ran for the woods along the river.

Buckner slammed on the brakes and the car skidded halfway through a full circle and then the dust clouded up around them and poured in through the open windows and filled the cab of the Cutlass.

Jewell swatted at the gritty air.

"Did he mean to do that?" she shouted.

"He's fucking running, isn't he?"

"Shit."

She undid her belt, threw her door open, and took off after him into the trees.

Jewell was an all-conference cross-country runner in high school, and still jogged almost every day. The boy had a head start but she didn't think it would take long to close the gap.

He was running toward Crooked Tree Park where there were trails and a bridge across the river, but there was only one direction for him to go until he hit the crossing. If he left the trail he'd be slow through the trees and she knew that land better than anybody on earth, outside of Lucy, maybe, and Buckner was waiting in the Cutlass to catch him if he spilled back out onto the road.

She kept to the trail and worked herself into her long stride and caught her first glimpse of him about a quarter mile from the bridge. If he crossed, she'd have him hemmed in quick. The Boogie Down Barn was on the other side of the river and there was nothing there but a single road that dead-ended at the club.

Delos must have known better, or guessed right, because he did not cross the bridge but took the park trail instead, and that complicated things.

The park trail would lead clear back to town, and she was worried he'd slip out into the woods somewhere and disappear entirely. Buckner was out of the equation now, and when she turned onto the trail she patted her pants pockets and they were empty. She'd left her phone in the car and now it was down to a foot race.

The boy did not slip out into the woods but kept on the trail and kept his lead on Jewell. The little fucker was fast and seemed to know how to run, too—he deployed his skinny arms in wide, smooth swings and rode his long strides like a pro.

Endurance would come into play shortly, though. They'd already run close to a mile, and she was on him now. She was close enough to shout for him to stop, but he did not even give her a glance over his shoulder—if anything, he picked up speed.

They fell into a rhythm. Both of them were topped out, or at least she assumed the boy was in a similar position to hers—running as fast as she could short of an all-out sprint. Jewell had put herself about fifty yards behind him and sometimes she felt like she was gaining, and other times she felt like he was pulling further ahead.

The Harbor North Resort bracketed the trail. There was the golf course and the condos along the river, and now Delos was running toward the single-family mansions and the big hotel on Lake Michigan.

There was another golf course there at the other end of the trail, the resort's marina, and guarded, gated entries. Jewell played private poker games on occasion down by the marina and could not imagine that Delos had any idea what he was running toward.

Still, she wanted to get to him before they reached the black gates. She wanted to avoid the commotion and potential security involvement, all of which could lead to the police and an entirely different scenario than they had imagined when they set out that morning.

Sunlight shafted on the trail through the high canopy and

there was bull thistle on the trail's edge and moments when she could see a swath of the big lake in the distance. They were nearing the resort, and much faster than she would have liked.

She screamed his name now, but he just kept running and never looked back. She gritted her teeth and pushed into her final gear, a full-on sprint, and Delos must have sensed her making her move because he shifted seamlessly into his own sprint and her thighs began to burn and her knees recoiled at the impact of the pavement through her New Balances.

The trail ended at one of the resort gates and now they were in the full wash of the sun and she could hear the sounds of traffic and the faraway drone of a beachside radio.

Delos did not stop at the gate but ran right past it. She thought he might be trying to circle the entire resort—at the moment, she would put nothing past him—but instead he took a hard left onto the gravel service road and began to wind his way into the resort from the back.

She gained some ground on the turn, but he still had thirty yards on her, maybe more, when the service road spilled into the maintenance area and he began to weave through the vans and the facilities trucks and was angling toward the marina.

There was something happening at the resort. There were people gathered on the big lawn around the docks and she watched in disbelief as Delos ran headlong down the second pier and leapt over the side of a lake yacht and disappeared into the boat.

Finally, she stopped running. She put her hands atop her head and breathed. She walked slowly toward the boat and believed she had finally, decisively, cornered him.

darnette

Darnette was discharged at nine that morning and arrived home to discover that Davenport, the international man of mystery, had somehow gotten into his house and left an envelope with $1,500 in cash on the dining room table.

He picked up the envelope and counted the money twice.

"Fuck me running," he said.

He should have driven right to Kendra Simmons's place to get himself fitted out for the hunt, but fifteen hundred in greenbacks was too big of an opportunity to waste and he had a feeling that if he could just reinvest that money in the slots, up at the casino, he might not have to go and hunt this wolf at all. He could give the cash back to Davenport, keep the profit, and go on with his life, or he could choose to take the job because he wanted it, and not because he needed it. This could be seed money for an investment rather than payment for services rendered.

He was going to the casino, that had been decided, but he did struggle a bit with what to wear. He couldn't find a T-shirt that sat right on his body, that was the problem. He was broad across the shoulders and chest and he liked the way T-shirts popped a little beneath his traps, but there was still the matter of his paunchy belly that needed to be resolved.

He had aims on a push-up regimen in the clink, but he never got that started because he was embarrassed to get down there on the floor in front of the whole jailhouse and show off his spotty form and poor conditioning. Hell, he might drop himself flat on the concrete and bust his nose if he wasn't careful, as out of shape as he'd let himself get.

A lot of political radicals made great use of time in prison in the movies. They came out hard of body and sharp of mind, but Darnette, if anything, had gotten in worse shape inside and hadn't read any books, either, though he was not opposed to reading in principle.

Finally, he decided to put on a hoodie to go with his blue jeans. He might be too warm, but at least he wouldn't be self-conscious, and he thought confidence was important when a man played the slots.

People said slots were a sucker's bet, but Darnette believed that a self-assured man who put his hand on the lever and pulled was much more likely to walk away a winner than one who was worried about how his belly looked while he stood there gambling.

There was never any question, however, about what he would drive. Darnette still had his old Ford from his flooring business, and though he hadn't worked in some time, he still felt good behind the wheel, and it was a lovely day to boot. The sun was high and the light was flaxen and easy over the hardwoods and the hills and he rolled his window down and hung his arm outside to swim it through the wind and he really did feel like this was a day in which anything at all could happen.

Darnette spent three hours on the same two rows of slots inside the Golden Eagle Casino. He started off hot, too. Ran his 1,500 right up to 1,800, then stalled out and dropped back to 1,200. He clawed his way quickly back to 1,650, but then came the big drop all the way down to 375.

He took a break then and sat on the stool in front of one of the Lucky 7s machines and began to wonder exactly what Davenport meant by two fingers. Was that a literal threat, or more figurative?

He wanted to think it was a colorful bit of hyperbole, but deep down he understood the proposition was literal. He'd only known Davenport for a matter of minutes, but it didn't take long to put together that he was a serious man and not likely prone to careless musings. The real question was, Which two fingers were on the chopping block, and would Darnette have any say in their selection?

This was a huge question he was disappointed in himself for not resolving. The difference between a pinky and a pointer finger was obviously vast, and when he said fingers did that also include thumbs? Darnette didn't think it should—the thumb was clearly a higher cut of digit, first class to coach as far as the hierarchy of the hand was concerned—but it wasn't like there was an international tribunal where he could appeal the ruling if Davenport wanted the big one. It seemed reasonable that thumbs were not included in the deal, but he should have clarified that first.

Still, even if he didn't take a thumb, there was no way old Davenport was going to be satisfied with a pair of pinkies, so what Darnette thought was most likely was a sort of structured deal. Port takes a pointer finger, then says, *Get me the money by Monday and your other hand is free to go. Get it by Tuesday and it's a pinky. Any day after Tuesday and I'm picking the digit.* Something like that. An incentive-based program.

Then again, Darnette thought, as long as I win the money back I don't have to think about any of it. He dropped another dollar in the machine and pulled.

It did get scary for a minute. He dropped all the way down to eighty-two dollars before he ripped off his hoodie and went full T-shirt. He wasn't too uncomfortable in the hoodie—casinos ran cold—but he needed a change of energy and it worked: He hit a triple bar on a two-dollar bet with his belly in the wind and suddenly he was on a roll.

He worked that same machine all the way back to nine hundred and for some reason when he got to nine there was a little voice that told him now was the time to cut his losses and he did. He pushed himself away from the machine and damn near sprinted out of the casino and into the afternoon.

Yes, he was down six hundred dollars and he'd wasted some time, but in the grand scheme it was closer to a no-harm, no-foul situation than the disaster he'd been staring down at eighty-two dollars.

He left the Golden Eagle and only allowed himself one more stop before he headed to Kendra's—Tom & Dick's party store for a cold six-pack of beer.

All in all, things were off to a decent start. He was nine hundred dollars richer than the day he'd walked into jail and still stood on the brink of great opportunity, and so he decided to take the positive view of things and rolled his windows down and turned the radio up.

"Only the Good Die Young" was on.

Normally, Darnette didn't care for the piano man, but old Billy Joel had a few good ones and this was one that Darnette enjoyed a fair amount. It was about trying to talk a girl into losing her virginity, which was one of those universal themes that spoke to relatable elements of the human experience and he tipped his head back and sang along with the chorus.

"You got a nice white dress and a party on your confirmation!"

Darnette meant to have a beer on the way, but ended up drinking two, and after forgetting to eat lunch he had a halfway decent beer buzz as he walked up Kendra's drive and gave her trailer a knock.

She came to the door in a Detroit Red Wings tank top and a short blue-jean skirt. Her blond-brown hair was pulled up with a scrunchie, and frizzy strands of it framed her face as she leaned against the door and looked him over.

"What do you want?"

He held up the rest of the six-pack.

"Just came by to say hello."

"The hell you did."

"I'm here to get fitted for a project but thought there was no need to keep it too formal. Figured we could have a beer together, as old friends, if you were so inclined."

"We're not friends and never have been."

"You say potato."

She went to close the door but Darnette pleaded.

"I need your help," he said. "And I got a shitload of cash. I just figured you and me could hang out for a minute in here, then head over to the pole barn and do some shopping right after."

"How much cash?"

"More than enough to make it worth your while."

Kendra looked him up and down.

"I thought you were in jail."

"I just got out this morning."

"So, that's what this is?"

"It's not only that, I promise."

Kendra turned around and walked back inside, but left the door open to the screen. The sun was still high and bright, and out in this part of Porcupine, in the low country, there was nothing but rocky fields and no shade as far as the eye could see.

Wouldn't be any problem to kill a wolf out here. Put a wolf in one of these fields and Darnette could hit it twice on the run, but wolves didn't like wandering around flat, open country. Wolves were smart and they were difficult to locate and even more difficult to shoot if you did. They were fast and they were elusive and it would be a challenge even for a hunter of his renown.

Kendra still hadn't invited him in, so he called out to her inside.

"So, what do you think?"

She was in the kitchen, banging dishes around the sink, but called out to him over her shoulder.

"I guess come in."

Afterward, they sat on the couch. She lit a cigarette and offered him one, which he accepted.

"You're smoking menthols these days?"

"They're Bill's."

"Who's Bill?"

"My ex. We split up last week, but he left a carton in the freezer."

"These things will tear your lungs up."

"Yeah," she said. "But they're free."

"So what's new?"

"Nothing," she said. "I'm still waiting tables at Duffy's. Taking some summer classes at the C."

This was Cutler County Community College, the C being both an abbreviation and a reflection of the school's perceived mediocrity. "Your Future Today" was their slogan.

"What are you majoring in?"

"It don't work like that up there," she said. "We don't have majors, per se."

"What are you wanting to be?"

"Maybe a teacher. Or do massage therapy."

"Are the classes hard?"

She shrugged.

"Compared to high school?" he said.

"I don't know. I can't really remember high school because I was so wasted all the time. I can tell you: Don't ever take psych with Ms. Moore, she's a total freak. But now I've got Jack Conner for abnormal, and it's awesome."

"What's abnormal?"

"Abnormal psychology," she said, and shot a few perfectly circled smoke rings.

"What's that? Like serial killers and shit?"

"Not really. Mostly it's about diseases of the brain."

"I take it your forays into education have not led you away from your other interests?"

"I got so much shit in that pole barn right now, you wouldn't believe."

"I need something particular."

"Let me guess, you want some wolf shit?"

"You heard I was on the case?"

"No. I heard everybody is on the case. They had some stupid town hall a couple of days ago and everybody is all riled up. You need to get while the getting is good. Brian Harse was out here yesterday talking about it. He said he saw tracks behind the Crow River and had pictures on his phone. Then somebody else said he just got those pictures from the internet and is trying to impress the ladies with them."

"Were you impressed?"

"I was not, as a matter of fact."

"You said the tracks were behind the Crow River?"

"That's what he said. Then others said he was full of shit. Then I heard somebody else say that he wasn't full of shit at all. They saw the tracks down there themselves."

"Where are you hearing all this talk from?"

"Well, I run a guns and ammo shop so I hear some throughout the course of the day, but it's all over Facebook, too. It's all anybody is talking about."

"Where on the river?"

"The tracks?"

Darnette nodded.

"Past the resort. Right there where the river runs slow and before you get to town."

"You know that for sure?"

"I don't know anything for sure. I'm telling you what I hear and what I read on the internet."

"Shit."

"What?"

"That's right near Sawbrook property. Nobody mentioned that to me."

"Who are you doing this for?"

"Some asshole that works for some other assholes."

"And they're paying you?"

"I wouldn't do it if they weren't."

"How much?"

"A lot. But they didn't say nothing about any Sawbrook land."

"They'll shoot your ass for trespassing up there."

"I know they will."

"At least Rhoda would have. I don't know about the kids. Buckner is a hothead, but I hear he's sober now."

Darnette mashed out his cigarette on top of his empty Budweiser and dropped the butt inside the can.

"Anyway, I guess we should go see what you got."

"I think you just did, Darnette."

She winked, stood up off the couch, and they walked outside toward the pole barn.

Kendra did not have a dedicated section for wolf hunting,

but she did have a fair amount of accoutrements and supplies specific to the purpose. The barn was lit with hanging panel lights and they were bright and buzzed loudly above them as Kendra pulled things from her handmade shelves and sat them on a long folding table.

The barn smelled like grease and gunpowder, it was a comforting scent, and Kendra held up a green cylindrical tool that looked like a miniature softball bat.

"This here's a wolf howler. It will do your alpha call and your lonesome call and you can do barks or pup in distress."

Kendra put the instrument to her mouth and demonstrated a few of the calls.

"How do you make the different sounds?"

"You just blow them that way. You wanna make a bark, then bark. You want to howl, then howl. You wanna do a pup in distress, hit the high notes and put some yelp in it."

"So you don't have to hit different buttons or anything?"

"It's not a goddamn trumpet, Darnette. Just make the sound you want and it will shoot it out into the woods, and if they hear it, they will approach."

"I'll take it."

"Damn right, you will."

"What else you got?"

"You fit for rifles, right?"

"Yeah, I'm all good there."

"How are you on night vision?"

"I don't have any."

"Well, you'll need it. You can't go hunting these bastards during daylight, now can you?"

"'Cause they're nocturnal?"

"Well, that and they're a federal fucking crime to hunt in Michigan, Darnette. You know that, right?"

"Yeah, yeah. I got that."

"So you need some night vision?"

"I guess I do, yeah."

Kendra picked up a pair of goggles. They looked like binoculars but were attached to a strap that she slid over her head. She held up her hands and wiggled her fingers and moved her head sharply from side to side to demonstrate the stability of the harness.

"Hands free."

"Nice," he said.

"You got a nightscope?"

"No, ma'am."

"You'll need one of those, too. For sure."

"How much is all this going to run me?"

"It won't be cheap, but we'll do a package deal. Can I ask you something?"

Kendra still had the goggles on and she stood looking at Darnette.

"Shoot."

"What do you got against this wolf?"

"Nothing. It's just a job."

"So it's just for the money?"

"One hundred percent."

"That I can understand. I don't agree with it, necessarily, I just intellectually get the motivation."

"You favor the wolves?"

"I like a fair hunt. I believe in fair chase."

"Half your business is poaching."

"Sure," she said. "But that don't mean I agree with it. And these wolves are just living the way God or whoever intended. They're not doing anything other than what they should do."

"I don't disagree."

"I respect them, I think. They're beautiful."

"Have you seen one?"

"Just in movies and on T-shirts."

"Oh," he said. "There's another thing I need. A pack to carry it out. I'm going to need to take it somewhere and deal with the carcass."

"Deal with it, how?"

"It won't be for wolf steaks, I can tell you that."

"You're going to disappear it?"

"That's what they told me, yeah."

"That's kind of sad."

"Maybe so, yeah."

"All right, let's find you a pack and then I got to get back inside and study. We got a test tonight in abnormal."

"Study the bold words," said Darnette. "That was always my approach."

"It don't really work like that in college, dude. At this level, things are more conceptual in nature."

The two of them walked across the barn toward a separate set of shelves. Kendra ran her finger over one of the display tables.

lucy

Lucy spent almost three hours watching Kendra's property, and then another two once Darnette Lewis arrived because he took so damn long.

He disappeared into the trailer for a solid forty minutes, then they both emerged from the back door and walked together toward the pole barn. Seemed they might be a little bit of an item, and Lucy could only hope they didn't procreate and tip the world's scales a little further in the wrong direction.

She didn't like Darnette, but he was a helluva hunter and she did hold a small amount of begrudging respect for his talents. He probably got his first buck when he was eight or nine years old and hadn't looked back since. She knew he'd bagged an elk or two along the way and had a reputation for tracking acumen and accuracy from distance. And he had all the motivation in the world for this poaching gig.

Darnette used to have his own flooring company and he did good work. Probably the first call anybody in northern Michigan would make if they wanted new hardwood put in, or old floors brought back from beneath a bad choice of carpet. He'd put out his own shingle and had two trucks on the road within his first two years and then the resort came in and everything boomed just right, at least for a minute, and then the boom got too big and the developers brought in corporate contractors.

Darnette didn't take a job when the big companies offered. He fought the good fight, but they put him down with low bids and quicker turnarounds and he wound up underwater within eighteen months and had to sell his second work truck and all his equipment at staggering losses, then he drank through a job at the Home Depot, and now he wasn't working at all. Now he was mostly just getting drunk and doing stints in the county jail for general foolishness and sporadic outbursts of violence. It was a story as old as time, and when he finally came out of the pole barn with a black duffel bag dragging heavy at his side, she decided to follow him.

She'd already pissed the day away staking him out, and didn't see any reason not to do a little recon before she headed back to the property.

Darnette left Kendra's and drove straight to the Paradise Junction bar, and she could only sigh at the predictable symmetry of his small-town ruin.

The Paradise Junction was a small concrete building without windows that sat in a gravel lot in a field about halfway between the Porcupine and Cutler County lines. There was no reason at all for the bar to exist in that specific place—it was an empty field exactly like every other field that surrounded it—and yet there it was, because it always had been, probably always would be.

There were three vehicles parked and she slid in beside

Darnette's work truck. Kenny, the bartender, was outside smoking a cigarette and he nodded at Lucy when she walked up.

Kenny had been in Jewell's grade in school and she remembered seeing him in the school production of *Brigadoon*. Jewell was on the stage crew and Lucy had gone to see it with her daddy. Kenny's Tommy Albright had stolen the show. He was a capable dancer and singer, but she thought he'd really soared in his scenes with Fiona. She couldn't remember the name of the girl who'd played Fiona, but she did remember thinking she had real talent. She remembered being impressed with them both.

Kenny smiled at her now.

"What you doing out here, Lucy?"

"Kind of in the neighborhood and just had a thought about a cold beer and here I am."

Kenny seemed suspicious of the explanation, but shrugged it off.

"How's Jewell?"

"The same."

"The same as what?"

"I don't know. She's just Jewell. How are you?"

"Shit, I'm terrible." Kenny nodded back toward the building. "Look where I'm working."

"It's not that bad," she said. "Is it?"

"It's that bad and worse. You can get sepsis just breathing the air in there."

"Figured you'd be in Hollywood by now."

"Ha!" he said. "I wish."

"You did a helluva job in *Brigadoon*. You really crushed it."

"Thank you, Lucy Sawbrook. That's nice of you to say."

"I'm not saying it to be nice, I'm saying it because it's true. What was that girl's name that played Fiona?"

"Allison Beckworth," he said, a touch dreamily.

"She was good, too."

"She was hot is what she was."

"What's she doing now?"

"I have no idea. I know she went to college but she never accepted my friend request on Facebook. Maybe she's in Hollywood."

"Maybe," Lucy said.

Kenny flicked his cigarette out toward the road and pulled the door open for Lucy.

"You still running the park?"

"I think that park is running me, Kenny. But yeah."

"First beer's on me. What'll you have?"

"Gimme that Banquet beer, Kenny. And I appreciate it, greatly."

"Least I can do for a fan."

"I bet you had plenty back in your day."

They walked inside together and then split off at the bar.

"I might've had a couple," Kenny said. "But they're getting harder and harder to come by."

Lucy took a stool and scanned the room and saw Darnette sitting at a table in the corner by the jukebox and the bathrooms. Kenny brought her the Coors and she said it had been nice to see him and left a ten on the table as a tip and walked back toward Darnette.

He looked at her as she neared, and she could see him trying to place her, and when he recognized who she was it surprised her that it triggered a smile.

"Lucy Sawbrook?" he said. "What in the world?"

"Darnette," she said. "You mind if I sit?"

He stuck out his hand toward the empty chair across the table.

"What brings you here?"

"I saw your truck outside and figured I'd pop in and say hello."

He took a drink from a bottle of Budweiser. She could see him processing that she'd come in just to see him. Could see him doing the math on what she could possibly want, and then landing on it directly—probably when he noticed her shirt with RANGER stitched across the front pocket.

"Because we're so close as friends?" he asked.

"Sure. Why not?"

"How's the park?"

"It's like any job. A bunch of bullshit between me and what actually needs to get done. Pay is pretty shitty, but I get to be outdoors and nobody is breathing too hard down my neck."

Darnette pointed his bottle at Lucy.

"See, I loved working for myself. That was always the prize to me, not having anybody to answer to."

"That's why you took on the big boys?"

"That's right. Couldn't imagine going back to having somebody barking out orders at me. Telling me where to go and when."

"I respected that. I still do. I was rooting for you, Darnette."

"I was rooting for me, too," he said.

"Might be some work for you right now, though, in another field."

He squinted at Lucy, like he had no idea what in the world she was saying.

"What's all this, now?"

"I hear there's some people looking to hire out poachers to try and get this wolf that has everybody so up in arms."

"Where'd you hear that?"

"Shit, where didn't I hear it? It's in the wind, man. It's everywhere. And I figured, if they were going to bring in a hired gun on this, I can't think of anybody better than Darnette Lewis."

"Are park rangers cops now, too?"

"No, we are not."

"Then why do I feel like this is an interrogation? 'Cause I just sat down to have a beer at the end of a long day."

"Long day doing what?"

"That would be none of your business, Lucy."

She took a drink of her Coors. There was a poster of a swimsuit model on the wall, part of a Saint Patrick's Day promotion, and it'd probably been hanging there twenty years judging by the woman's hairstyle—all choppy bangs and curls and crimps.

Darnette was leaning back in his chair now, waiting.

"I don't like poachers, Darnette."

"Well, if I see any I'll let them know."

"You know what a poacher says when they shoot a wolf and get caught?"

Darnette glanced around the bar, like it was a game show and he was crowdsourcing the answer.

"I don't know. *Oops*?"

Lucy arched an eyebrow. The answer infuriated her, but she didn't want to give him the pleasure of a reaction.

"Basically, yeah. They just shrug their shoulders and say they thought it was a coyote. Who's to say, right? Not much profit in prosecuting that kind of crime and everybody sort of goes on about their business."

"See, that makes sense to me," said Darnette. "I mean, end of the day, most folks aren't losing any sleep over a dead predator. It all comes out in the wash."

"Exactly. Which sort of has me wondering about what would happen in the case of a poacher getting shot."

Darnette didn't smile, but he didn't seem bothered, either. If anything, he appeared to be amused by the suggestion.

"Hypothetically," she added.

"I think that would be murder, wouldn't it?"

"Maybe. Or maybe, if somebody were stomping around my property, or my campground, all fitted out like it was the end of days, and here it is August, not even rifle season for crying out loud, a person might not be faulted for thinking it was a criminal of some sort. One of those mad gunmen."

She paused for Darnette, but he just gazed in the direction of the bar and took another gulp of beer.

She went on.

"In these days and times, who could blame a person for thinking along those lines? Shit, put a bullet in a man like that, and I mean a kill shot, not some sort of leg wound, just put a man down where he stood, and they'd probably call me a hero for it. Put my name on a park bench."

"God, it almost feels like you're trying to threaten me, Ranger."

"I don't think I'm trying to, Darnette. I think the trying part is over."

"I remember a time you were considered the sane Sawbrook."

"Being the sanest Sawbrook doesn't mean you're not crazy, Darnette."

"Except I don't think you really are. I think you might talk that way on occasion but when it comes down to it, I just don't know if I see it."

"I came here to tell you not to do whatever it is you think you're about to do. I came here for my own conscience, so if the time comes and you put me in the position, I will not hesitate. I will put you down, Darnette."

"Over a goddamn wolf?"

"It's not just the wolf, Darnette, though that might be enough if I'm being completely honest. At the end of the day, yeah, I'd probably take a wolf over you. All things being even. But it's bigger than all that. It's just that at a certain point you have to take a stand and say what it is you can and can't abide. And I don't think I can abide somebody shooting at a gray wolf because they feel their right to build another goddamn golf course is being infringed upon by an entire species having the gall to survive. I think that's just the spot where I've decided to draw my line."

"Shit, Lucy. If there's one thing we both know, it's that

people like you and me don't get to draw the lines. We just got to walk between the ones that are already there."

She stood up from the table. Took another drink and then left the bottle half full on the table.

"I guess that's just where you and me are different, Darnette. I didn't lose one fight and shrug my shoulders and give up. I'm going to keep drawing my own lines, no matter who tells me I can't, or how difficult it may get."

jewell

Jewell never took her eyes off the boat where Delos had disappeared. He was too slippery and too quick and she could not risk so much as a sideways glance at the marina or he might wind up swimming halfway to Wisconsin.

There was a real crowd gathering on the big, open lawn at Harbor North. There were tents set up and people milling about and music playing through standing speakers. It was an art festival—local painters and jewelers peddling their wares to the summer tourists who loved a little local culture, particularly if they never had to leave the resort to acquire it. There was a squad car at each gated entrance for security and several food trucks were parked just beyond the gates.

Jewell walked out onto Pier 2 and all the way down to the lake yacht where Delos had hidden. The boat sat hunkered down alone at the end of the dock, and while Delos had leapt over the side, she took the stairs onto the boat and spat his name with as much anger as she could fit inside a whisper.

"Delos!"

He did not respond and she crouched lower and made her

way toward the middle of the boat, though to call it a boat struck her as ridiculous.

Boats could be driven by little old men in floppy hats. Sometimes, they could even be paddled. Her own family had bought and sold many boats over the years, a half dozen probably, and this was nothing like anything she'd ever seen, let alone stepped foot in. This was a vessel, something that should have been named after an admiral or whatever senator secured its funding.

She entered the galley first. There was a microwave and stove and sink and a dishwasher and full cabinets and a wine tree. The counter doubled as a cutting board and there was a table and cushioned swivel chairs and through the galley was a room twice as big as the kitchen. She was sure they had some ridiculous nautical name for such a place, but it was, for all intents and purposes, a lounge.

Inside, there was a couch and two recliners and a mounted television. The furniture was all cream colored and the walls were paneled in dark wood, and she opened two closets and peeked behind the chairs, but there was no Delos.

The boat rocked gently and the sound of the water lapping off the dock posts was steady and slow. She put her hands on top of one of the recliners and was about to circle back toward the front of the boat when she saw a small crack of light from the floor.

There was a hatch right beneath her. The top was not fully closed and she pulled it open to find a short staircase that led to sleeping quarters—two twin beds and small port windows and a soft string of lights that circled the room where the walls met the ceiling.

The boy was sitting with his back against the headboard and his face was smeared with tears, and when she saw his bottom lip start to quiver she went and caught him in her arms just before the sobs came.

The boy cried and, when he had to breathe, told her in fits and starts what happened. He told her how he'd stolen the rifle and thrown it in the quarry and that he would be sent back to Woodyard but that he didn't know what else to do because he had felt certain that Mr. Baker was going to shoot the wolf and kill it.

"What do you mean, go back to Woodyard?"

"I was there for six months. It's a prison—"

"I know what it is. That's no place you want to be."

He shook his head.

"No, ma'am. I don't want to be there and I won't go back. Not ever again. I can't stay with you all but I can't go back to county, either. They won't even have another hearing. I'll be right on the van back to Woodyard and I can't do it. I just can't."

He was so skinny that when he sobbed his whole body shook and she held him and absorbed his tears the best she could.

"I'm sorry," he said. "I know I fucked up."

"Why didn't you tell us about the rifle? Or Woodyard?"

"Because I wanted you to like me."

"We do like you. Maybe we didn't make that clear enough. But either way, you got to tell us the truth about things. You have to let us know what's going on so we can help you."

The boy sniffled.

"Okay."

"I left my phone in the car," she said. "There's no way to get ahold of Buckner and I saw two squad cars out there. Did you see those?"

"No, ma'am."

"Do you think the police are looking for you? Would your foster parents have called this in? Tell me the truth, now."

He nodded.

"Yes, ma'am."

"You got to stop calling me ma'am. We're probably related and my name is Jewell."

He lifted his head off her shoulder and wiped at his eyes.

"So you believe me? About being kin?"

"I already pretty much believed you, but now that you've run off and made everything so goddamn difficult I know it for a fact. You got to be a Sawbrook to cause this much mess."

The boy's eyes were puffy from crying and his face was streaked with dirt where he'd wiped the tears with his hands. He was wearing a plain black T-shirt and the same ragged, cut-off camo shorts he had on when he jumped the falls. He smelled like sweat and the river and she knew he would stick out like a sore thumb with the resort crowd. She wasn't certain she could sneak him out, and without a phone, even if they made it outside the gates they'd be stuck in the wide-open and still a few miles from home.

She thought they should sit tight until the art festival ended and then sneak out the way they came in. Maybe when the sun began to drop a little above the bay and the day wasn't quite so bright.

"I think we got to wait it out. At least a little bit. Maybe get out of here after this festival thing."

Delos leaned back against the headboard and cast his eyes down, away from Jewell. He looked frightened and ashamed, and she was more sorry for him than she was angry. At least at the moment.

"You're a fast little fucker," she said. "Do you run cross-country?"

"What's that?"

"You never heard of cross-country?"

"No, but I haven't heard of lots of things."

"It's a footrace through the woods. It's a team sport, but you can get individual prizes, too. I ran it in high school and made all-state."

"Wow," he said.

"You should try it. You'd be great at it."

"You just run through the woods?"

"Basically, yeah."

"It sounds kind of easy."

"It's easy if you're good at it."

"I'm sorry for running. And for not telling you about the rifle."

"That's okay. Just don't let it happen again."

"I won't."

"You promise?"

"Yes, ma'am. I promise."

"Then you got to promise to stop calling me ma'am."

"That's what Buckner said, too."

"Was that before or after you went over the falls?"

"He said it before, but wanted me to stop right after."

"Were you afraid?"

The boy shrugged.

"Buckner shouldn't have done that."

"It's all right."

"He told me you jumped off that ledge."

"I did."

"That was stupid."

The boy looked up at her and smiled and her heart just about melted when he did. She reached out and tousled his hair.

"You and me will be fine, Delos. As long as you tell me the truth."

"Okay."

"Are you tired? Because you sure as hell look it."

The boy nodded. The boat rocked gently from side to side, and before long, Delos let his eyes slide shut.

Up close, she could see how young he was. The hard, tiny pimples on his cheeks and across his forehead, and the faint beginning of a mustache above his upper lip. He was skinny and lanky, but his cheeks were full and rounded.

His breathing steadied quickly and he seemed to be asleep, though she noted he'd appeared that way in the car as well. There was no door for him to roll out of here, though, and she left him in the sleeping quarters and went up the small staircase.

She walked back through the lounge and the galley and onto the deck and she looked back toward the shore. The squad cars were still parked at each entrance and now there was a barricade by the maintenance area where they'd come in, and the crowd had only grown.

It was afternoon and the sun was beginning to float west. The light was canted on the lawn and she drummed the boat railing with her fingers and felt a little too conspicuous outside of the covered quarters.

She made her way back toward the boy, but stopped in the galley first and opened the fridge. Helped herself to a cold Labatt and grabbed a bottle of water and a Dr Pepper for the boy and climbed back inside the hatch.

Delos was sleeping hard now. He was breathing slow and in rhythm and she tucked a pillow beneath his head and put his drinks down on the nightstand.

Jewell sat on the end of the bed with her beer and twisted off the cap. She looked out the port window at the line of the water and she watched it rise, then gently drop.

darnette

Out in Lakeview Heights, Darnette was traipsing through a half acre of marshy woodland behind Sheriff Dunn's house. It was just a little cedar swamp outside a subdivision, but it was swarming with mosquitoes and Darnette had blood smeared across his palms from where he'd squashed the little bastards on his neck and forearms.

He'd come straight from the Paradise Junction after that little shakedown from Lucy Sawbrook and demanded to speak with the sheriff. Parked his truck right out in front of the sheriff's place, which was two stories and new construction with a two-car garage and pitched roof. He had a sprinkler set up on the lawn and an actual white picket fence. Darnette gave the doorbell a good, long ring and the sheriff damn near blanched full white when he saw who was standing on the porch.

"What the hell are you doing here?"

Dunn was talking through the just barely cracked door.

"We need to talk."

"The hell we do."

"It is important and it is urgent."

"Get the fuck off my porch," Dunn said. "Are you crazy?"

"Crazy, how? I'm just stopping by on my way home from work."

"You don't have a fucking job and we're not friends."

"I'm just saying that we need to talk and it's not that big of a deal."

"If you want to talk to me, you can get your ass to the roller rink, park out back, and I'll meet you there after dark."

"No."

"What do you mean, no?"

"I mean no. No means no. Or haven't you seen the commercials?"

"I don't have time for this, Darnette."

"I don't either," he said. "Which is why I'm here."

"What do you want?"

"To talk!" he said. "In a respectful manner."

"We can talk at the roller rink."

"We can talk here, or we can talk not at all."

Sheriff Dunn leaned his head against the door and closed his eyes.

"You want to talk here?"

"Yes, sir, I do. I believe I have earned that right. I'm not one of your narcs that you like to chat up at the roller rink."

"You haven't earned jack shit, but if you feel so strongly about meeting on my property, then take that truck and park it behind the roller rink and walk through the marsh and I will meet you at my back fence. If you choose not to leave this porch and do not move your truck right now, I will call two deputies to come and arrest you for trespass and harassment."

"Fine," Darnette snapped. "I agree to your terms."

Now he was standing on the other side of Dunn's back fence, arms and legs hot and itchy with tiny red swells and the bugs still biting. Sheriff Dunn reeked of insect repellent and spoke to Darnette through a space in the plank wood fence.

"I'd like to come inside," said Darnette. "I'm uncomfortable and I've been bitten to shreds."

"What is this fixation with my house?"

"It's not a fixation. It is a desire."

"A desire for what?"

"I would like a cold beverage and to sit in your home as an equal as we discuss matters."

"You and I are not equals. We never have been and never will be. What the fuck is all this about?"

"Can I at least have some repellent? These fuckers out here got teeth. The skeeters."

"I'm not giving you my spray. You're likely to run off with it."

"Just squirt some through the cracks, goddamn it. Mist me."

Dunn grumbled some obscenities to himself, but he did put his little spray bottle up to the fence and gave a few generous spits of bug spray that Darnette held up his arms to receive.

"How about something a little higher. For my face."

"Fuck your face," Dunn said. "Talk or leave. What the hell is this about?"

Darnette took a breath. He deplored the way the sheriff spoke to him and the petty ways he wielded his power, but there was too much at stake to get bogged down any further in Dunn's microaggressions.

"This is about some information I have come across about where this wolf is and me needing to talk to your associate, the resort guy."

"You can't talk to him."

"Why not?"

"Because that's not how this works."

"That wolf is on Sawbrook property and I was just threatened by none other than Ranger Lucy herself. She harassed me while I was out at dinner and threatened to shoot me dead if I stepped foot on her property."

"How did Lucy get all hooked up in this?"

"I have no idea, but she's damn serious about that wolf."

"You can't just go talk to these resort people. It's not how it works."

"This guy, Davenport, he's not the one paying me, is he? It's not his money, right?"

"I don't know."

"Yes, you do."

"No, it's not his money. "

"He's just a heavy, right?"

"He's a little more than that, but yeah, basically."

"Well, I'm not asking to talk to his boss, whoever that is. I'm not saying I need a sit-down with the sultan, I'm just saying Davenport needs to let those people know the price of this job has just gone up because nobody said anything to me about where this fucking wolf was."

"Nobody knows where it is."

"I think Lucy Sawbrook does, otherwise why is she shaking me down at the Paradise Junction?"

"You said you were at dinner."

"They got peanuts."

"Look, I don't know what terms you agreed to, but if you want to ask for more money I can't stop you."

"Can you give me his number so I can shoot him a text?"

"Absolutely not. That's a hard no on that, Darnette."

"I'm assuming if I don't get paid on this, neither do you."

"I'm not blowing up my business relationship with the man over this, but yeah, there's some incentive for me to get this done."

"And I'm not doing it unless he bumps my pay."

"Look, short of giving you his number, which I'm not doing under any circumstance, who's to say you couldn't bump into him at a public event? Something like the hoity-toity fundraising brunch they're having down there tomorrow."

"At the resort?"

"That's right. A couple of the superrich families are putting it on and I'd imagine he might be there as some sort of security. Blending in, but being a presence, too. Maintaining the sort of delicate balance his work requires."

"What's the fundraiser for?"

"I don't know. Who fucking cares? Save the whales or kill the porpoises, what does it matter?"

"How would I get in there?"

"Shit, I don't know. You've got to figure that part out yourself."

"What time is it?"

"I don't know, Darnette! I wasn't invited! I didn't get anything in the mail requesting my RSVP. I'm trying to be helpful, but there's limits to what I can actually do."

"So just sneak in there and try to bump into the man?"

"That's my suggestion, yes. My other suggestion is that you never come back here to my house again, under any circumstance, for any reason. You do that again and I might just shoot you on sight."

"That seems extreme."

The sheriff turned and made his slow way back toward his house. His waddle was as pronounced and wide as ever.

"Night, Sheriff," Darnette shouted.

He waited for a moment, but Dunn didn't answer. Darnette tried not to take it personally, but he did.

jewell

Jewell woke up to the drone of the boat engine through the hold walls, though she did not know that it was an engine right away. At first, she was disoriented and couldn't tell you her name, but then she saw the boy, still asleep on the bed, and remembered him rolling out of the car and the chase down the trails and climbing onto the boat.

She looked out and the water was so dark it was like the portholes were buried beneath heavy, wind-tossed curtains. She shook Delos by the shoulders and the boy blinked his eyes open and she watched him take in his surroundings and realize where he was, the same way she had just done. He started to say something and she put a finger to her mouth to hush him.

"We're moving," she whispered. "Somebody is on the boat."

The engine was a low drone and the walls around the bed were vibrating, but she could hear voices and some music, too. Not music so much as a series of heavy bass drops.

"Sounds like a party," Delos said.

She looked at the boy and could see that he was calculating. His eyes were darting back and forth across the small room—he was looking for an escape route and it appeared he was slowly coming to recognize that none existed.

Jewell put her hand against the wall and it wasn't vibrating so much as it was shaking.

"I feel like we are going very fast."

"How far out do you think we are?" he asked.

"We could be pretty far out. Or maybe we're headed back to the dock. Could be either one."

"You think we might be headed back?"

"Probably not, but maybe. I don't know. I'm looking out the same little windows you are."

"Are you scared?"

"I'm not comfortable with the situation," she said. "I can tell you that much."

"I'm sorry I lied and that I ran. I shouldn't have done that. I should have just told you about the Bakers and the rifle."

The lights were low in the sleeping quarters but she could see how wide his eyes were open, how sincere he was when he said that he was sorry.

"It's okay," she said. "We're past that now."

"Are we just going to wait down here?"

"Unless you've got another idea, I think that's the plan."

"I don't have any ideas at all. I'm through with having ideas."

"I doubt that," she said, and pointed to the water and the Dr Pepper she'd stolen from the fridge. "Those might be warm by now, but they're for you."

He reached for the Dr Pepper first, unscrewed the top, and had a long gulp. He offered her the bottle, but she shook it off.

She grabbed the water instead, took a quick drink, then handed it to Delos.

"Have this," she said. "We may be stuck here awhile."

"I got to piss already."

"That's what the empties will be for, if it comes to it."

"What happens if we dock somewhere else? Like what if we don't stop until we get to Canada or somewhere?"

"No matter where it is, the second we can get off this boat that's exactly what we're going to do."

He took a drink of the water and she thought maybe she could climb the steps to try to get a sense of what was going on topside—but as soon as the idea formed, the hatch-door flew open and the air that poured in from above was fresh and cold and it broke the seal of the engine drone. She could hear the voices and the music more clearly now, and she could see the high sprays as the boat careened across the open water.

There was a man at the top of the stairs, shouting. He'd already seen them and without a word Delos bolted off the bed and tried to escape up the ladder but the man dropped a foot and kicked him square in the head, and she shrieked when the boy went limp and fell backward. He landed hard on the floor, unconscious, and she ran to him and shouted his name.

The boy was breathing but he was not awake and she felt a yank on the back of her shirt and she was being pulled up the stairs and each step slammed hard against her back and hurt very badly and everything began to swirl together into a stew of panic and anger and pain and she saw sudden flashes of light and movement.

The wind was hard and cold, even in the room above the

hatch, and there were several men standing over her and they were loud and they were drunk and when she tried to stand, one of them pushed her back down with a foot.

This was a different foot than the one that kicked Delos. Boat shoes instead of sneakers. The men were talking about stowaways and joking about what pirates would have done and then one of them said something about drawing straws for turns and somebody else said they should manage it like a batting order, and the men laughed.

She understood what was happening. One of them was straddling her and she could smell something metallic and medicinal on his breath, something chemical he had smoked, and his dark eyes were narrow and the whites were all shot through with blood.

She turned her head and tried to wriggle free and saw a life preserver hanging from one of the dark, paneled walls. It was blue and said CREW MEMBER in gold stitching. A second man was pinning her arms to the ground while the man above her was unsnapping his pants, and she turned her head and saw Delos at the top of the stairs and he was holding her Labatt and he swung it at the man on top of her.

The bottle shattered against the man's skull and there was an explosion of glass and beer, and when the man who had her arms pinned reached for the boy, he swung the broken bottle and cut the man clean across his face. There was blood running in bright streams down the man's cheeks and neck, and he screamed and fell.

Delos reached for Jewell and she grabbed his hand and they both ran onto the deck and then toward the stern. The boat lurched hard, once, and she almost fell but steadied herself and climbed atop the railing, and the air was even sharper now beneath the wide night sky and she did not look back to see if the men had given chase but planted her feet and pulled the boy along with her and leapt.

That was the moment she realized how far out they were—when she saw only black water around them and how it was flat as glass beyond the wake and shone with all the bright stars above it.

The water was cold and deep but Jewell sought it. She wanted to put as much distance between her and the boat as possible and she made herself long and kicked her legs beneath the surface, and when she finally came back up she tried not to flail or gasp for air and looked for Delos.

She saw an arm waving on her periphery and swam for it but did not shout.

The next time she came up for air the boat was nearly out of sight and she could no longer hear the engine. Now she called Delos's name but he did not answer.

She could see splashing but could not see his head and he was further away than she had thought; she swam in a full sprint and did not stop or draw air until she felt his shirt and clutched it in her fist and flipped over on her back.

She asked the boy if he was okay, if he could swim, but he did not answer. She pulled him up out of the water and set his back against her chest and he choked on water and coughed and she held him there and they floated.

"I can't swim good," he said.

"What does that mean?"

"It means I can't swim at all."

The lake was calm, but it was lapping over Delos's body above her and she had to turn to the side to try and find a breath.

"You can't swim?"

"No, but I can float some."

They bobbed for a minute. The boat had not come back and they were well beyond its wake and the sky and the water both bled together and blurred at the edges of Jewell's vision.

"I need to catch a breath. Can I slide you off for a minute and just see if you can float? If you can't float I'll pull you right back up."

"Okay."

She noticed his body was shaking.

"Are you afraid?"

"Shit yes, I'm afraid."

"Okay, I'm right here. I just need a few breaths and then right back up, okay?"

"I already said okay once. You're the one that's hesitating."

She slid him off and took a deep gasp of air and let her body relax. He was rail skinny, but it was still a hundred-plus pounds of body weight she'd been carrying.

Delos was on his back beside her and kicking his legs a little frantically and she told him that it was okay. He reached out his hand and she held it and took one more breath before she pulled him back up and tried to steady her back beneath him to keep them both above water. They drifted together for a moment. Finally, she caught her breath.

"How'd you grow up here and not learn to swim?" she asked.

"It's been difficult," he said.

The lake was briny and seemed to have grown even wider and darker around them. Jewell realized they could have been halfway to anywhere by now, but there was no way of knowing and she could not see land or light of any kind in any direction.

She tapped Delos on the arm to let him know it was time for another break. He nodded and she slipped him off and breathed, and this time he did not let go of her hand but just let himself go under the water while she took her breath, and when she was done she brought him back up.

There were a million stars stretched above them and the longer she looked at them the closer they began to seem. She had her arm around Delos's belly and he held her hand in his own and they floated.

Jewell was tiring fast. She would fight with everything she had but she knew there was a place she would reach where her will would no longer be of any consequence, and she feared that place was nearing. She could feel her energy spilling into the lake and her muscles beginning to tighten and grow heavy.

Delos gave her hand a tap and he slid off and she breathed. She took one full breath and then another. She let her chest fill with air and then she brought Delos back up and they floated.

She had no idea if they were moving in a particular direction or floating in circles, but when her head banged up against something solid, she saw it was a rock that extended above the water and she shouted Delos's name and did not wait for him to respond or to say that he was ready. She did not wait to discuss a plan or ask him for his input but just shoved him in the direction of the rock and he reached out and grabbed it and pulled himself up with his back arched and his legs chopping hard, and he scaled that wet stone surface like a lizard.

Now he was atop the rock and reaching down for Jewell and she swam to him and grabbed his hand, but when she tried to set her own feet against the rock it was slick with moss and she slid back into the water.

"How'd you get up there?"

"I don't know, really."

He reached down and they tried again and this time when she fell backward she banged her elbow hard against the stone. Delos was still reaching for her, and the third time she grabbed his hand he started to fall and she let go quickly and dropped. She thought Delos would be falling, but he put both his hands beneath him to stop his slide and then scurried back up.

"That's enough!" she shouted. "Just stay up there. I can swim."

"Swim where?"

She leaned her top half against the rock and treaded water with her legs. Her shirt was torn and she pulled it off over her head and tossed it up on the rock.

"Wave that if you see anybody. I'm going to swim for a bit. I'm just going to go out a little bit and see if there's any land. This rock means we might be close to shore. Doesn't it?"

"I don't know. I don't really know the water like that. I hate this shit."

"Every twenty seconds or so just call my name so I can find my way back. I won't go too far and then I'll come back. Does that make sense?"

"You want to try and get up here again first?"

"I don't think I can. Let me do this, and if I can't see anything, then maybe we'll try again. But promise me, you stay up there unless I come back and tell you different. Okay?"

She waited, but Delos did not respond.

"Fucking promise me, dude. Do it right now."

Delos turned his head. He was really considering the promise, which meant he took his promises seriously, which was admirable. On the other hand, she was treading water and waiting.

"That's the shore right there, I think."

He was pointing to his left and she turned but could not see beyond the few feet of water in front of her.

"That's the shore, Jewell. I can see it. I'm pretty sure that's it right there."

"What's it look like?"

"It's like a line with some bumps in it. It's different than the water, though. It's a little lighter. The color of it."

"I'm going," she said, and put her feet against the big rock and pushed off in the direction the boy had pointed.

She made a conscious decision to cut loose, to not try to conserve energy, to advance so that if it was the shore she could get there before she had to try and float any longer. If it wasn't land, that might be a mistake, but it was a calculated risk and probably the right play, considering.

She dug hard until her arms went to pure Jell-O and then she closed her eyes and dropped and hoped to feel the lake bottom beneath her. If she could just reach a sandbar she could walk far enough to save enough energy to make the last push.

She made herself narrow as she fell. She fell and she fell and she fell. She fell so long she was just about to give up and kick for the surface when she felt something whisk at her toes. She dropped a moment longer, but when she did not find footing she had to rise quickly and when she hit the surface she gulped for air and she could hear how desperate she was to breathe, and it was her own panic that frightened her the most.

She swam again. Dug hard, again. She chopped water until she could not feel her arms at all, and when she dropped it seemed like she fell even longer, like she was trapped within the narrow walls of a nightmare, and now she felt nothing at all beneath her—not even a whisk of seaweed—and her chest began to smolder and her lungs felt thin as paper, and when she surfaced she flipped on her back and floated and gulped for air.

She had one more push in her and she swam and dropped and this time she felt the first brush of slimy lake bottom quickly. Her feet were in the thick muck, but the water was still above her head. She bent her knees and sprang upward, and reached with both arms for the surface and felt her lungs go flat again. Then her right calf twitched and clenched itself into a cramp, and when she screamed she took on water, kicked her left leg, pulled with her arms and reached, but she could not find the surface. It felt like it was falling away from her, maybe for the last time. She kicked again and finally broke the surface, and when she gasped and screamed it was a single sound and she flipped over one final time and let her leg go crazy with the cramping and treaded the water beneath her with her arms.

The next time she dropped, the water rose no further than her neck and she planted her feet in the lake bottom and breathed and she could see the shore not twenty yards from where she stood.

delos

I hadn't promised anything to Jewell on that rock because she'd told me not to lie to her again and I did not aim to let her down. She wanted me to sit there and wave her T-shirt around for help, but what she didn't realize was that I didn't want any kind of help if it led me back to Woodyard. I'd have lived on that rock forever before I went back to Woodyard, and I knew damn well I couldn't make it to shore on my own by swimming.

I'd watched Jewell for as long as I could see her, and she went at least twice as far out as I would make it. And I didn't want her coming back out after me, either. I thought she might, too. I could see her getting to shore, resting up, and then swimming all the way back. Or she might go someplace and call for help, and if help came, that would be it for me.

So I stayed crouched on that rock and ready, and scanned the water for anything at all that I might float on. I thought about the Sawbrooks, too. The crazy shit I'd read about survival out in the big, open water. I told myself that I was one of them and that I could make it if I tried, and even though I didn't really believe it, it was better than thinking I wouldn't.

When I saw a piece of driftwood about ten feet from the rock, I steadied myself in my crouch. I watched it float for a moment and I couldn't be sure if it was coming closer or moving farther away, or if it was even a piece of driftwood at all. It could have been anything, I suppose, a piece of clothing or some rubber, but the way it seemed to be on the top of the water was enough to convince me to try.

I came up out of my stance and leapt with everything I had and I reached out my arms and I swear I was up there like a heron—pure wide wings and altitude—until I dropped.

I landed square on the target and plunged beneath the water with it pinned to my chest. I didn't know what it was I'd landed on. At first, I just went under and heard the water roaring in my ears and felt my body dropping and I didn't know if I'd ever come back up until I kicked my legs and the driftwood sprung to life and lifted me along with it, and when I broke the surface I found myself floating on a big, square piece of solid wood. I pulled myself up so that half my body was above the water while I kicked my legs behind me and started to move toward the line I'd seen in the distance that I was nearly certain was the shore.

part III

lucy

Lucy and Sky drove to the Boogie Down Barn around one in the morning. Delray had texted and said they had four sewing machines for the fladry but only three girls able to work them after close, and Lucy said she'd be there.

She wasn't going to sleep, anyway. It was like Jewell and Delos had up and vanished off the face of the earth. She and Buckner had both driven from one end of the county to the other, then back, and there was not a trace of their sister or the boy to be found.

The good news was that neither of them had called from jail or the hospital, and Lucy thought the boy had probably run somewhere he shouldn't have and now they were both holed up and hiding until they could make a break for home.

Sky took Frog to her mom's and Buckner was going to stay on the property in case they showed up, and while Lucy was no fan of the Boogie Down, she was glad to be out in the night with her sister-in-law.

The Boogie Down Barn stood at the end of a two-track off a road with no name. It was a converted pole barn in the middle of a pine clearing where the cars parked on gravel and grass and aligned themselves in makeshift rows. The night was clear and there was light from the moon and from the pink neon glow of the sign above the door. *Enter*, it said, above an arrow pointing down.

Inside, there was one stage, two poles, and a homemade plywood bar. There was a folding table for the deejay, and the smell of sawdust and stale beer was soaked into the walls and the warped wood-plank floor.

The ceiling was exposed and there were several small communities of chickadees and finches that nested in the rafters, and while they occasionally dive-bombed the stage or a patron's table, they could largely be trusted to stay above the fray during working hours.

Sky had been the Barn's most popular performer—this was where Buckner had fallen in love with her—but she hadn't been back in the year since she retired. There were hugs with the bouncers and the dancers, and when they went to get a beer from the bar, she was set upon immediately by Teddy Ralston.

"Sky? Is that you?"

Sky asked for two beers and smiled at the short, stocky man on the stool beside her.

"Hey, Teddy."

He looked at her in true and actual awe.

"You are a vision this evening. If I may say so."

Sky was in a black tank and blue jeans and had her hair pulled back in a ponytail.

"Teddy, I haven't even taken a shower."

"And yet my heart burns."

"Sounds like you need some Tums."

"Let's start with this Long Island," he said, and lifted his drink to his mouth. "See if this doesn't do the trick."

Teddy was a retired hedge funder and, in a room of problem drinkers, he had the purple-hued, bulbous nose the rest could point to as the hallmark of true alcoholism. He tried to pay for Sky and Lucy's beers but Sky waved him off just before the stage lights came down.

The fog machines discharged their purple-pink mist and the first splash of saxophone hit the speakers. There were catcalls from the audience and Jennifer Cart strode on stage just as the bass dropped on "Rump Shaker." She'd cut right to the chase, too, and come out topless.

"Spoiler alert," said Teddy Ralston.

Sky took Lucy by the hand and led her to the back of the barn where they leaned against the wall with their beers and watched Jennifer dance.

To the right of the stage Lucy could see there were four sewing machines set up in a row and then she turned and saw Delray approaching, his Hawaiian shirt as loosely buttoned as ever, his chest hairs all bristly and white and far too close to her face.

"You made it!"

Delray reached out his hand and fist-bumped Lucy, then Sky.

"Don't even bother to ask me to come back to work," Sky said.

"Because you already decided you would?"

"Because I'm trying to enjoy myself and don't want to remember the fact that you used to be my boss."

Delray looked at Lucy.

"I'm a great boss. Which Sky knows."

"Don't tell me what I know and what I don't, Delray."

"Anyway," he said, "we miss Sky every day but are also glad that she's moved on and found happiness in life. Even if it's with Buckner, which none of us can understand."

"Nobody understands it," Lucy said. "Trust me."

"So," he said. "You guys are going to stay after and help with the fladry?"

Lucy drank from her beer.

"That's the plan."

"Good. I'll show you the draft I wrote of your post afterwards, when we have some quiet. I've already posted it on my blog, but gave you credit as the author and named myself the editor."

"Anyway," Lucy said, "I do appreciate you doing this."

"Like I said, we're all on the same team."

They were rounding the corner into the second chorus of "Rump Shaker" now and Jennifer crouched on the stage and suddenly the spotlight swung to the bar, where Teddy Ralston was standing on his stool, and the rest of the room turned to him and then the music stopped and the Barn sang along as he delivered his line on cue.

It's Teddy, ready with the one-two checker!

The room erupted, the music returned with a hard, low bass kick, and Jennifer strutted across the stage to raucous applause.

Lucy looked at Delray.

"Oh," she said. "Because his name is Teddy."

Delray wagged his finger at her.

"There you go."

There were thirty-some men at the tables up front, and a handful more with Teddy at the bar. They were mostly golfers and resorters—regulars in polo shirts and visors—their sunburned necklines more dark than bright close to summer's end.

There were two tables of locals as well, and Lucy asked Delray how those two separate groups got along with each other.

"They get along great, because I make sure of it. It's one of my strategic principles."

"Here we go," said Sky.

Delray held up his hands in protest.

"You know it's true, you used to bitch about it more than anybody."

Lucy looked at her sister-in-law and Sky acquiesced.

"It is kind of true. But it's the way he goes on about it that's so annoying."

"You treat the locals with the same attention as the resorters," Delray said. "They don't tip as well, of course, but if the girls ignored them there would always be trouble. Locals are naturally predisposed to resent vacationing wealth and the last thing they need is to experience the very dynamic they might be trying to escape in their real life in even sharper relief when they're trying to have a good time at the end of a long workweek. It's smart business, but it's also the right thing to do. Yes, I'm a businessman, but first and foremost—"

"He's a local," said Sky. "Delray Harper is first and foremost a local and I've probably heard him say that five hundred times."

"And it's been true every time. Just like it's true for you, and for Lucy. And you know who else was a local, long before us? The wolf. The fucking wolf was one of the first locals to get driven out of here and we're going to make damn sure it doesn't happen again."

Somebody shouted Delray's name from a table near the stage and he excused himself and left, but not before he reminded Lucy to check with him after close about the rewrite.

Lucy drank from her beer and turned to Sky.

"Does he ever stop?"

"Not ever, not even once."

"Rump Shaker" had faded out and the music had stopped and the stage was empty and dark. The deejay, Lyle Soulveski, said that everybody was in for a treat because Jennifer was going to give a special performance tonight and asked that the crowd remain quiet.

Sky pointed at the stage.

"I heard she was doing this tonight. This is why I wanted to come when we did."

They'd killed the fog machines up front and Jennifer had put on a flowing skirt over her G-string and a billowing, caped blouse. She had on a black stovepipe hat and heels and stepped onto the stage and stood to the side of the spotlight, and there was a loud round of applause. She ducked her head and waited for the cheering to subside and then the Barn grew so quiet that Lucy heard the clap of Jennifer's heels as she walked to stand center stage in the spotlight.

There was a catcall from the back of the room and Jennifer slid down the pole so that she was sitting facing the audience, then she dropped her head into her folded arms.

The music started and there was a piano playing softly and Jennifer rolled into a few floor moves, and then a man's voice was singing "Mrs. Potters Lullaby" above the piano and a drum-beat and Jennifer sat up with her hands behind her and she shoved her chest forward and dropped her head back.

Lucy turned to Sky.

"Is this the Counting Crows?"

"Yeah. It's the really long one. She only does this like three times a summer."

There was a loud burst of clapping and Lucy turned back to the stage, and watched Jennifer finally stand and fling her hat into the crowd. She grabbed the pole and spun, and then began to ascend to the top, where she inverted and threw her legs behind her. One split moved to the next and they were both paced and inseparable from each other—a constant motion, all swirls and slicing kicks.

She landed finally in a Russian split. Both her arms and her forehead were against the pole as she stared up, her right leg to the pole beside her face and the left pointed arrow straight into the crowd. The girls had gathered to the side of the stage and they shouted her name and there was more applause from the crowd.

Jennifer returned to the floor, walked to the back of the stage, trotted to the front, and leapt onto the pole. She melted into an invert and she spun and spun and spun and spun. She trailed her blond hair so fast behind her that it seemed to sit perfectly still and straight, and when she came out it was on the strength of a single arm as the other held the back of a foot, and she rose into a half bow. The other dancers watched her wide-eyed and adoring, and Lucy realized she had tears streaming down her cheeks and she could not exactly say why and she did not need to know. In that moment, if she could have made the dance last forever, she would have.

Jennifer was above them all now, near the rafters, and her body was draped over the pole beneath her and her head had returned to the same forward repose she'd begun in and the music went down and the room rose to their feet, but she was not done yet.

Lucy wiped at her eyes and there were a few more beats of silence and then the music returned and Jennifer dropped from the pole, and the moment she landed, her hat was flung from the side of the stage by one of the girls and she caught it cleanly and flipped it on and remained bowed until the music returned and her head snapped up and the man sang, "Ah, you can see a million miles tonight, but you can't get very far."

The chorus returned and the fog machines kicked on and the room erupted in cheers, and if the pole barn had burst suddenly into flames, not a single person there would have been surprised or even sorry that it had happened.

jewell

Jewell and the boy sat on the rocky shore together as the sun rose. She had been walking back into the water to retrieve him, her own piece of driftwood in her arms, when she saw him kicking his way in from the sandbar.

She had helped him in, though he didn't need it by then, and they'd both collapsed in exhaustion on the shore when it was over. They slept, and when Delos woke in the cold, gray dawn, he took his shirt off, wrung it out as best he could, and draped it over Jewell like a blanket. Shortly, she blinked her eyes open and sat up beside him.

"You saved my life," he said.

The sun was coming up behind them and the sky above the water was still pocked with stars. There was mist above the reed grass in the shallows and the waves crashed hard beyond the sandbar in the distance. There was a strong wind and they were both cold and knew they would have to get up soon and walk for help, but they needed just a few more moments to rest.

"You saved me, too," she said. "You were incredibly brave."

"I'm sorry I can't swim."

"Well, you're going to learn. I'm going to make sure of that."

She stood up and reached down her hand to the boy. He took it and she pulled him up and then they both turned from the water to face the land behind them.

The shore was rocky and the birch and the pine came on quickly, and the forest was newer growth near the water, where the trees were short and set wide. Between the trees was sand and light dirt, and they began to push back into the woods.

The boy asked where they were.

"Shit, I have no idea."

"Could this be Canada?"

"I think it's more likely the UP, but that's just a guess."

They walked side by side. Jewell had put the boy's T-shirt on and both of them had kicked off their shoes and were barefoot. There were fat black flies and mosquitoes and they both slapped at their skin, and there were bright-red smears where they caught the insects with a clap.

"I'd kill to be at a card table right now," she said. "Cold, complimentary beverages and a comfortable chair. Air conditioner churning and the jingling of the slot machines like chimes all around me."

"I've never been to a casino."

"Good. You're too young."

"How good are you?" he asked. "At poker."

"I'm good enough. I've got a little shtick I use that helps."

"What's a shtick?"

"It's like an act, I guess. I tell all these crazy stories about my family and about Cutler County in general. Tourists like to play against me and lose."

"Are the stories true?"

"True enough."

"Can you tell me one?"

"Someday, yeah. They take a while. I do a whole setup. Create a sense of the time and place. Do a little backstory when it's needed. Unless I'm telling a story about Rhoda, my mom, in which case I don't have to make any of it up."

"What was your mom like?"

"She was the best person I've ever known, and occasionally also the worst. She didn't answer to anybody and apologized for nothing. For better or worse."

"Can you tell me a story about her?"

"I could tell you a hundred, but I stopped telling Rhoda stories after she passed. I need a little time with that."

"Do they make you sad?"

"A little bit, but mostly it's that I don't know which ones I want to give away yet. I want to keep some for myself, some special ones I don't just give over to the tourists for a couple of bucks."

They walked along together, the boy taking in every word Jewell told him. Then he slowed his pace just a tick and shook his head.

"I can't believe anybody likes to lose at cards."

"It's hard to imagine, but it's true. It helps to think of me like a tourist attraction. I cater mostly to golfer types, but I've had some couples on date nights, too. Things like that. It's just a whole different world of people. They got so much money, they won't ever go broke. They got their money invested and out in the world. We work for money, they got their money working for them. It took me a long time to figure out what a difference that was, between the two ways of living."

"I guess my shtick was telling kids I was a Sawbrook."

"How so?"

"In county I told this kid Randy about being a Sawbrook, and I said that if he kept stealing my desserts then I would call on the Sawbrooks and they'd come and whup his ass."

"And that worked?"

"Pretty much. Randy started giving me his dessert sometimes. Do you think you could teach me to play cards?"

"As soon as you learn how to swim. That's number one on the list, no questions asked."

The sky above the trees was blueing with light and the sand had become dirt and there was milkweed and purple thistle among the tall stalks of waxy grasses and sedge. The air was beginning to warm and the edges of their shorts were drying.

"So, how close were you to the wolf?" Jewell asked. "The first time."

"Five feet. Maybe a little further, but not much."

"And he just stood there?"

"We both did."

"That's really cool, Delos. My daddy would have loved that. He talked a lot about how we were connected to animals. He'd see deer or a bobcat in the wild and take all kinds of meaning from it. I can't even imagine what he would have said about a gray wolf, though. The first one in this county for over a hundred years? Maybe he wouldn't have said anything at all, maybe that would have been too amazing to him to even speak on."

"When I first saw him here in Cutler, I didn't know if it was real or not. Me seeing the same wolf in those two different places so far away, it seemed like something I would imagine.

Or maybe there's more than one wolf. But once I saw him again, I don't know, I just knew for a fact that it was the same wolf. I felt it in my gut."

"You're connected to that wolf, dude. I don't know how, or why, but you are. Did you ever read about Alfred Sawbrook? The first Sawbrook up here? Way back in 1850? He was like an expert tracker and trapper. A great woodsman."

"I read a lot about him. He was a fur trader and he communicated with the whites and Indian tribes. Spoke a bunch of languages and bought up a bunch of land. I did a whole report on him for English class when I was in Woodyard."

"My mom would have loved you for knowing all that history on your own, Delos. She would have given you all the land she gave to me, Lucy, and Buckner and told us to pay you rent. Have you ever seen the display they have on him in the museum? Alfred?"

"No, I've never been to the museum."

"Well, that's third on the list, then. After swimming and cards."

"Are you really going to teach me how to swim?"

"Yes. That is one hundred percent happening."

"They don't have a swimming pool in Woodyard."

"I know that, too. But you're not going to Woodyard, Delos. That's one thing I've decided for certain. As long as you answer me one question first."

The boy looked at Jewell and his eyes were big and unblinking. She could see how badly he wanted to answer whatever she asked, and the stark depth of his wanting put a pang in her heart.

"Okay, here it is. What I'm wondering is, if you knew you were our kin for all this time, why didn't you ever say so until now?"

She could see the boy searching his thoughts. She wanted to put his mind at ease, to tell him to relax, but she also wanted the truth. He looked up at her.

"My mom said you were bad people, but what changed my mind was seeing the town hall where Lucy and Buckner spoke up for the wolf. So that's part of it."

"What's the other part?"

"I didn't want to find out if it wasn't true. I wanted us to be family so bad, I decided I'd rather not know for sure than find out it was a lie."

She wanted to hug him, but he was standing a few feet away and part of her felt like he might take off and run if she so much as made a move in his direction. That's how vulnerable and skittish he appeared. He'd answered her question in full, and he had left himself bare.

"That settles it, then," she said. "I don't know exactly what will happen, but I'm certain it won't be Woodyard."

"Really?"

"Yes," she said. "Really."

She was going to say something else, and maybe give him that hug after all, but Delos shouted and pointed up ahead. She turned and saw the barbed-wire edge of somebody's property and a sprawling, two-story house on the other side of the field beyond the fence.

The grass in the yard outside the house was freshly mowed and there was a pole strung up with an American flag and a green-and-white Michigan State University banner that fluttered right beneath it.

"Looks like we didn't quite make it to Canada," she said.

"You think we're in the UP then?"

"Probably so, but maybe not. Maybe we're somewhere in Porcupine County, but either way we're going to go up there and use the phone and call my friend Connie."

"You're not calling Lucy or Buckner?"

"Hell, no."

"Why not?"

"Because I don't feel like getting lectured for however long this drive is about to be. Connie's my best friend, and she'll just be glad we're okay, and probably stop to get us some coffee and donuts on her way."

"That sounds good."

"Doesn't it?"

"I take mine black."

"Of course you do. And if anybody asks up here at this house, your name is Fred Sawbrook, but we call you Freddie. You're my cousin and we were out on a Jet Ski when the motor seized up and we had to swim for shore. Something like that should work."

The boy stood for a moment with everything that Jewell had said. He seemed afraid to speak or do anything that could possibly alter the trajectory of the future she'd just suggested.

"You good?" she asked.

He nodded.

"Good," she said, and hoisted herself over the fence.

He followed.

darnette

Darnette was going to attempt to slip into the resort in his work truck. That's what he'd decided.

He'd try the service entrance and make up some story about how he was there to give an estimate, or maybe try an outright bribe if that was what was required. Or maybe he'd drop Davenport's name, just to see what happened. Call him Port to imply familiarity, and tell the security guard to call him up and interrupt the man at the fancy soiree if he felt that was the proper course of action.

Darnette might have gone bankrupt two years earlier, but he still felt a flush of pride and a little boost of confidence the moment he slid into the driver's seat of his F-150. Could still recall the very moment he'd rolled it out of the detailer's when he first went into business for himself—the white paint buffed to a high sheen and the red stencil lettering clean and bold on both doors.

LEWIS FLOORS
THE BEST IN CUTLER COUNTY

The phone number came next, with the old-school area code—231. Those were digits you either had or you didn't and Darnette flew them like a flag down both side panels of the Ford.

At his peak, Darnette had two trucks on the road and three full-time employees, but it was always his show from top to bottom. He did the books and he was good on a drum sander, and what separated him from the competition was his craftsmanship. He worked the finishing edges, did all the custom builds, and had a God-given eye for detail. But more than anything, it was his patience.

Outside of work, Darnette was a notorious hothead. Couldn't get through a Lions game without putting his fist through some drywall, but give him some high grit sandpaper and he turned into the Buddha himself. He possessed a nearly infinite capacity to focus on a single spot of wood until it flowered beneath his ministrations and was polished into the perfect shine and smoothness. It was what made him such a good hunter, too. Patience. Simple as that.

They must have still remembered him at the service entry, because they saw his truck and waved him in without a question, which was flattering. Or maybe they did that with all the work trucks these days. Darnette didn't know, he was not kept abreast of changes in Harbor North policy, and the only thing that really mattered was that he was through security.

Most of the resorters kept their cars in long-term parking and zipped around the grounds on golf carts, and Darnette's was the only vehicle on the roads inside the gates. He felt a little conspicuous, but it wasn't too far to the designated lot for maintenance vehicles, where he parked the truck and was glad to get out and stretch his legs and walk for a moment among the financial and social elite.

Turned out not to be much of a walk, though. The fundraiser was at one of the first mansions outside the service lot and just beyond a hedgerow so densely branched and towering that nobody on the other side could possibly be accosted by the visual presence of proletariat transportation.

The house itself was three stories tall and built on a ledge that faced the bay. There were plate glass windows that spanned two levels and marble steps and arched doorways, and Darnette walked up the staircase to the front door and pushed it open like he belonged.

Inside, the party was a sea of pastel shirts, liver spots, and sundresses. The home smelled vaguely floral and the chatter was loud, boisterous, and fast. Caterers weaved through the crowd with silver serving trays held above the fray, and Darnette found the general vibe welcoming. People nodded at him and smiled, and nobody asked him for identification, and he felt free to wander and mingle as he saw fit.

He did not see Davenport in the entrance area, but he did notice a man in a Hawaiian shirt who was waving in his general direction. Darnette looked behind him, but there was nobody there and the man nodded as if to say *Yes, you,* and Darnette walked over.

The man in the Hawaiian shirt was a short, roundish bugger with a bald head and he was standing with a group gathered by a big stone fireplace.

"Are you the maintenance guy?"

Darnette looked at the man. Did not know what to say. There was music on the stereo but it did not have words, which Darnette found vaguely unsettling. It was classical, of all things.

"Maybe I am," he said. "But then again, maybe I'm not."

Now the man in the Hawaiian shirt was stumped. Everybody stood there for a long moment and it felt like it might get awkward, as the man seemed unsure of how to proceed. Darnette felt like his cover was about to be blown, so he recalibrated.

"What I'm wondering," he said, "is why you're asking?"

"I'm asking because I put in a call yesterday about the kitchen door."

"What's wrong with it?"

"It's sticking," said the man. "It's supposed to swing both ways but it keeps getting caught in the frame and the caterers can't get through. So we've got it propped open and I'm standing here and all I can hear is the damn clanging of the trays and cutlery."

Darnette pointed at the door behind the man.

"This one here?"

"That's the one."

"Probably just swelled a little from the heat."

Darnette went to the door and stood on his tiptoes and could see where the wood bowed in the middle.

"That's exactly what it is," he said. "Just a little swollen."

"Can you fix it?"

"Of course I can. Just give me two minutes."

Darnette took the short walk back to his truck and opened the built-in toolbox in the flatbed. Just rummaging around felt like old times—the clank of the tools and the sense that something was about to be made better than it had been.

Darnette grabbed a planer, walked back inside, and asked the man if he had a step-stool or something he could get up on. Hawaiian Shirt grabbed one of the caterers and told him to get a stool out of the pantry and within a minute there it was—set down right at Darnette's feet. He nodded at the caterer.

"I'll need a broom and dustpan, too."

Darnette stood on the stool with the planer and shaved at the bulged spot and it felt so good—that back-and-forth motion and the sound of the tool scraping against the wood and how quickly that little swell was resolved.

Darnette hopped off the stool and tested the door, and Hawaiian Shirt gave a little shout of appreciation when it swung easily through its arc. The caterer had brought a broom and dustpan, and Darnette swept everything up quickly and ducked into the kitchen to dump the shavings. Then he came back out and shut the door behind him and sealed the noise of the help and their food preparation where it belonged—out of earshot.

Hawaiian Shirt closed his eyes and savored the quiet from the kitchen.

"My God," he said. "I didn't realize it was so loud until it stopped."

"Anyway," said Darnette, and went off to find Davenport.

Now he was walking through the middle of the party holding a planer. Turned out he felt more comfortable with the tool than without it, and he decided not to bother with another trip to the truck.

A caterer passed and he snagged a flute of orange juice off the tray, but when he drank it he discovered that the juice was mixed with champagne.

"What in the hell is this?"

"I'm sorry?" said the caterer.

Darnette held up his glass.

"This tasty little treat. I'm just wondering what it is."

"Uh, that is a mimosa."

Darnette cleared the drink, then put his empty glass on the tray and replaced it with a new, full flute. The caterer gave him a scolding look, but when Darnette didn't flinch, the server just rolled his eyes and walked away.

Darnette took his fresh drink into a small area between the living room and dining room where there were shelves and a sitting bench and an enormous splatter painting that covered the opposite wall. The room seemed to have no purpose but itself—it was a place that existed between two other places simply because it could.

The younger people were all outside. Darnette's age, maybe younger. Pretty girls in summer dresses and men in polo shirts and bright dress shorts. He wondered what they were talking about in their little circles of good fortune. Stock derivatives? Baseball scores? Gossip? Darnette drank from his flute, decided he didn't care.

Another caterer passed and Darnette picked a little pancake roll off his tray, just to prove he could. Tossed it in his mouth and was delighted to find a little sausage tucked inside. Well now, that was tasty.

He washed it down with a gulp of the mimosa, then cleared

the flute and grabbed another drink when the next tray came through. This was what being rich was like, he thought, a delicious sausage wrapped inside a fluffy pancake, endless fruity drinks, and all of it brought on a silver platter to a room with no purpose.

Wealth also meant paid security—black-ops henchmen with fake handles like Davenport, who grabbed him so hard by the elbow that Darnette nearly shouted. He didn't shout, though, because Davenport whispered "Quiet" as he pulled him across the living room.

Davenport practically dragged him up a narrow staircase that led to a hallway where he wrenched Darnette's arm behind his back and shoved him into a room and slammed the door shut behind them.

Darnette stumbled onto a couch along the wall and looked at the man above him.

"Jesus Christ, Port, what the hell, man?"

"What the fuck are you doing here?"

Davenport was wearing a pink golf shirt and khaki pants. He had on loafers and the same sunglasses he'd worn in lockup. He was very tan, but the skin was white just above his sleeves.

"I came by to see you, actually. I was hoping—"

"What the fuck are you holding?"

Darnette looked down at his lap.

"That's a planer."

"What the hell's that for?"

"I just fixed the door downstairs. You're welcome, by the way."

"So you came here to fix a door?"

"Obviously not."

"Then what?"

"It's the fact that you're going to need to pay me a helluva lot more money if you think I'm wandering up into the Sawbrooks' property to get this wolf of yours."

"What are you talking about?"

"The wolf you want me to kill."

"Do you know where it is?"

"Pretty much. And what I'm saying is that the risk has increased significantly and we need to renegotiate the parameters of our deal in the light of this new information. I was threatened yesterday by the park ranger herself, Lucy Sawbrook. She said she'd shoot me between the eyes if she saw me on her property."

Darnette let that information settle with Davenport and glanced around the room. He hadn't had a chance to take in his surroundings with all the commotion and threats and general rudeness.

This was another interesting space. There were nautical maps on the wall, like regular maps but for rich people, and the floor was dark oak and there was light through the big windows in the wall behind him. The room was comfortable, yet serious. It was a place men went to drink whiskey and discuss things. Maybe women, too, in this day and age. The floors were well done, which was painful to acknowledge, but also true.

"Did you track this thing yourself?" Davenport asked.

"More or less."

"What does that mean?"

"It means I did my recon and I'm comfortable with the findings."

"Where did the park ranger threaten you?"

"At the bar. The Paradise Junction."

"What were you doing at the bar?"

"I was having a drink, dude, what do you think I was doing?"

"Why weren't you doing what you should have been doing?"

"I wasn't aware I was punching a clock on this."

"I told you time was a real concern. I told you that from the jump."

"You should have told me that I was going to have to deal with the Sawbrook jungle, too, and crazy-ass Lucy and Buckner and everybody else. That's what you should have told me."

"All right," said Davenport. "You might be trying to squeeze a little more juice out of this deal or maybe you're telling the truth, but I'm thinking that doesn't matter as long as you get this thing dead and buried by, say, tomorrow."

"Tomorrow?"

"Correct. I think it'd probably be worth it to my people to pay a premium for that sort of expediency. We'll go as high as twenty-five, but if the job doesn't get done in time, it goes right back to fifteen."

"No shit?"

"I don't say things just to say them, Darnette."

"But I got to get it done by tomorrow?"

"How many times do you want me to say it, Darnette? Would you prefer it in French?"

Darnette stood up from the couch before Davenport could change his mind. Stuck out his hand to shake.

Davenport slapped his hand away.

"Fuck you."

"Touché," said Darnette. "Which is French, in case you were bluffing just now about knowing the language."

Davenport exhaled dramatically. Rubbed his temples with his hands and then stuck his thumb in the direction of the door.

"Walk out the back entrance. Do not speak to another person on your way and never come back here again. I see you show up anywhere else you shouldn't be and I will take your ass out into the bay and drown you. I'll drown you and make it look like you got drunk and fell overboard."

"That's pretty specific," said Darnette. "That's, like, really detailed."

"That's because it's not an idle threat."

Davenport stepped aside so there was nothing but open space between Darnette and the door. Darnette had a notion to try and snag the last word on his way out, to say something smart to put a point on the board, but there was real money on the line and he'd already learned the hard way that pride didn't pay the bills.

buckner

Buckner had worried all night about Jewell and the boy. Lucy and Sky had run off to the Barn, which he didn't love but also didn't see the benefit in complaining about. He fell asleep on the couch somewhere around four in the morning, and when he woke, his phone was lit up with texts.

Jewell and Delos were safe and Connie was giving them a ride home. Connie had texted and said they'd be back around lunch, though she didn't say where she was going to get them, or what had happened. Lucy and Sky were still at the Barn, and Sky had sent him pictures of the sewing machines and the girls working and Delray sitting up on the stage reading something to his sister like he was some sort of poet on high.

He called Jewell, but then heard her phone ring and remembered she'd left it in his car and that was part of the reason why he didn't know where she was the night before.

He knew he could give Connie a call, but honestly, he didn't feel like dealing with Connie at the moment because she was probably still on her way to get Jewell and she might not know anything yet and she was not one of those you could just talk with to get information and then hang up on. Connie always had to go on about this and that and whatever the gossip was, and she was not very good at picking up cues in conversation that suggested you were ready to move on. Connie would just keep talking until Buckner wound up snapping at her or hanging up in a hurry and then he would feel vaguely guilty about it, which wasn't fair because why didn't she feel guilty for talking his ear off and not picking up on context clues and letting him off the goddamn phone?

In his previous life, as a drinker, Buckner would have been as rude as he wanted, and if he did feel bad about it afterward he could just get drunk and forget that it ever happened, or figure out a way to excuse his behavior or even blame somebody else for what he'd done wrong.

But now, in sobriety, you had to take your inventory, and when you were wrong you had to promptly admit it, and so you couldn't just go around all willy-nilly, making phone calls to people like Connie without being aware of the potential cost. Even if she might have information you desperately wanted, like what the hell had happened to his sister and Delos and where she was going to pick them up.

Buckner was already tired of thinking about the pros and cons of a goddamn phone call, and his sponsor, Dean, who he both admired and deeply detested, always said that if you were ever unsure of what to do in early sobriety, then apply the Hippocratic oath. That meant "first, do no harm."

The basic idea was that if all things were even, it was better not to act because in early sobriety you couldn't really trust your own instincts and choices. Buckner had googled the Hippocratic oath and learned it had to do with medical professionals and for a while he thought Dean might be a doctor, which seemed weird because of how poorly he dressed and how much he smoked, but it turned out Dean was a radio deejay, which made a lot more sense and was also a job that Buckner thought was very cool and that he didn't even know existed anymore. But apparently it did. Dean was a deejay for Double Rock KLT, and while he played the Stones too much for Buckner's taste, he did say some interesting, philosophical things sometimes between songs or commercials for used cars and discount furniture sales.

Maybe he should call Dean instead of Connie. Dean said to call when he was feeling good, so that it didn't feel difficult to call him when he was feeling down, and Buckner thought he'd brew up some coffee and do exactly that when Sky's mom texted him and told him to turn on the news.

There's something going on right there on the river. I think it's on your property. It's to do with Sovereign North.

Sovereign North was a Cutler militia outfit and Sky's mom was right, something was going on at the river. There were five men standing there all fitted out with their weapons of war and signs about their freedoms being encroached upon by the goddamn wolf.

They were not on Sawbrook property but were set up about ten yards from the line, and they were already all over the local news. Buckner called Lucy but she didn't pick up, of course, so he just went and got his .32 and his hunting rifle and drove off property and upriver. Didn't even wait to brew coffee, and damn sure didn't call Dean.

darnette

Kendra texted Darnette right after he left Harbor North, and said she had something to show him. He took it to be a sexual overture.

I would like to see you again but I got to get this job done tonight and I'm afraid I'd be distracted and not much good in the boudoir anyway. How about in a day or so?

Kendra did not respond for a solid ten minutes, so he followed up.

Boudoir is French for bedroom.

That one she answered, right away.

I know what boudoir means. This isn't a booty call. I got something that's going to help you on this hunt. That's what I'm texting about, dummy.

Well, that text turned him right on. Her straightforward,

no-nonsense nature. Darnette liked a take-charge attitude in a woman, not to the extent that it required leather and code words—he didn't plan to be crawling around on all fours anytime soon—but he didn't mind a stern order here and there, and she was the type of woman who would tell you what's what and not apologize for it.

On the other hand, time was short and Darnette felt pretty good about his gear. It was everything else that concerned him. The Sawbrook property was vast and beset with dangers and then there was the matter of actually getting a halfway decent look at the wolf and hitting him with the one shot he would have. Maybe two shots, max.

He'd watched a bunch of videos on YouTube, at least a half dozen, and everybody that had ever hunted a wolf liked to talk about how challenging it was—how smart the animals were and how difficult they were to hit once you did locate them. He wanted to see Kendra as soon as possible, for business or pleasure, but he just didn't have time to drive clear out to Porcupine County unless he knew for sure it would be worth his while.

Her next text settled the matter.

> I got drone footage, dude. I got the whole property mapped out and I got something else you're going to want to see. I'm at your house right now. Don't be weird about that. It's time sensitive and you need to hurry.

Darnette did not feel smothered or ill at ease about the idea that Kendra had shown up at his house unannounced—in fact, he was flattered.

Kendra had the latest in paramilitary technology and she had been thoughtful and considerate enough to deploy it in an effort to help him pull off what was beginning to feel like an impossible task. Drone footage could provide exactly the sort of tactical foothold he needed and he was more than touched by the entire thing.

She was waiting on his front steps with the laptop in hand when he arrived. They went inside and she flipped it open and got down to business.

He sat on the couch beside her and she didn't even seem to notice the general disrepair of the inside of his house—the dirty dishes and dirty clothes and various stains and chips and tears that accompanied the little bit of furniture he actually owned. Or, if she noticed it, she didn't seem to care because she'd already mapped the Sawbrook property on separate tabs and they were loaded and ready to roll and she pointed out the hills where she thought the wolf was most likely located, and then identified three separate spots where she believed Darnette could find a clear angle to shoot.

"Of the three," she said, "the biggest and best is right here."

She clicked on a clearing to mark it red and then connected it with a line to a pair of houses at the top of the hill.

"The problem is, it's close to where they live. That's the challenge, but look at those sight lines."

She traced around the edge of the clearing and clicked on other spots for comparison.

"This one here, by the house, that's a damn near guaranteed kill if you can get it there. Those other spots, even as good as you are, I don't put your chances much above fifteen, maybe twenty percent."

Darnette didn't know if anybody in his entire life had ever paid him such careful attention or been so capable and thoughtful in their assessment of the logistics involved in a hunt and how those applied to his particular skill sets. He was moved, and glad to have the assistance.

"The one thing about that clearing close to the house is I'd have to pack the wolf out. Couldn't bury him right there. Wouldn't have time and they'd find it anyway and blow it all up in the media."

She stared at the computer. Drummed couch cushions with her fingers and considered the problem.

"There's only one road on the entire property and you're right there beside it in the big clearing. Those other clearings put you too far out and that is some actual wilderness up there, and you're on their territory. They know it and you don't. You want to be close to that road, I think, and here's the other thing: I have two spike strips with me. I got them right out there in the truck. You take those and set them out and if they give chase it's going to wind them up in a ditch."

"You think I should drive right over there, by the river?"

"You're clear from the law on this, correct?"

"That's right."

"Then I think so, yeah. But the more I think about it, the more I think you don't want to fuck around with the night vision. What I've got is good—it's not military grade, but it's close enough."

"So what's the problem?"

"The problem is, it's still different if you've never worked with it before, and you've only got one shot at this thing."

"I think I can get two off, actually. I saw a video where a guy got off two clean ones."

"Okay, two. But that's it. That's the max."

Darnette agreed.

"For sure. Two at the most."

"They're going to come running. The Sawbrooks. They won't hesitate, but I still think you'll have time. Take both spike strips. Put one down close to the house, and the other close to the clearing. I'd give you more if I had them, but honestly, that should be enough."

"Did you bring those special, or do you just always have them handy?"

"I carry them with me in the pickup. In case of an emergency chase-and-evade situation. You don't think you'll ever need them, until you do."

"That's really smart."

She looked up at him from the computer.

"Thank you. My mom thinks I'm crazy."

"Nah, you're not crazy. You're just right."

She smiled.

"That's nice of you to say, but we need to stay focused."

She pointed at the computer screen.

"So, what do you think?"

"I think it's dangerous," he said. "No matter what."

"Yeah, it might be too dangerous. I don't know. I wouldn't judge you for calling the whole thing off. How much are they paying?"

"I found out about where the fucking thing was and told them to double down."

"And they did?"

"Not quite double, but yeah, they jacked it up a good bit. Didn't even put up much of a fuss."

"Good for you," she said.

Kendra closed the running tabs on her laptop and opened a web browser. She had that on 7&4 News, where the home page featured a picture of the Sovereign North militia standing near the Crow River. They had an entire arsenal of weaponry and big placard signs about the wolf and democratic freedoms. Underneath the picture it said DEVELOPING in big, red letters.

"What's this now?"

"This is a little bit of good fortune thrown our way. Sovereign North is getting involved in this wolf business."

"Are they trying to hunt it, too?"

"They can try all they want. Those aren't hunters, Darnette. They're just out there doing a show of force. Getting all fired up about rights and constitutional violations and whatnot. You know how they get."

"Oh, yeah. All frothy at the mouth."

Kendra pointed at the screen.

"But look who else is there, standing right across from them."

"Is that Buckner?"

"In the flesh. Which means now is the time to get over there and get yourself on that property. While they're distracted. Get up in the thick brush, off the road. You can get to the clearing when it gets a little darker. Just hunker down somewhere and wait. Go at dusk, like I said. Honestly, I'd drop you off and extract you myself, but I got class tonight and I can't miss it."

"You've really thought this through."

"I like to strategize."

"That's never been my strength."

"You have other strengths," she said.

"I guess maybe we make a good team?"

"I think maybe we do."

"You sure you don't want any money for those spike strips?"

"You just go ahead and take those, and once you get that wolf and get paid you can take me out to a nice dinner and we'll celebrate in style."

"Shit, this works out, you and me are having a steak dinner at the Golden Eagle and then we're hitting the slots."

"Whatever floats your boat."

Darnette looked at Kendra. Didn't quite know what to do with all the warmth and affection he felt in his heart.

"Oh, yeah. How'd that test go?"

"I got an eighty-six."

"Goddamn, congratulations."

"I was hoping for a ninety-five."

"Really?"

"That's my standard. I'm an A student, Darnette."

"That's pretty impressive."

"So is this thing you're about to do."

"Yeah," he said. "If I can do it."

"I've got a feeling you can," she said, and then leaned across her laptop and kissed him on the lips.

lucy

On the river, Lucy had arrived at the standoff to find her brother with a hunting rifle looped over his shoulder as he stared down six members of the Sovereign North militia that were standing across the dirt road.

The news trucks were on opposite ends of the scene and she parked behind the van from 7&4 and went to stand beside her brother. He pulled a .38 out of the back of his blue jeans and handed it to her. The afternoon was bright and hot.

"What the hell is all this?"

"This is a dipshit convention, Sister. It's a goddamn farce is what it is."

The militia was outfitted with AR-15s and they had pistols and tactical knives strapped and tucked everywhere that Lucy could see, and surely some places she had no interest in viewing.

The militia wore black T-shirts with images of skulls and eagles and fluttering flags, and they had on protective goggles and helmets. Hockey helmets and combat helmets, mostly, though one of them was in a Cutler High School football helmet with the face mask removed.

"I was out at the Boogie Down all night. Me and Sky were. Working on the fladry."

"How'd that go?"

"Good. Really good. We about got it done and then Delray saw this on the news and told me about it. I haven't slept a wink."

"Where's Sky?"

"She's done at the Barn and went out to get her hair done. Delray's having a big thing at the Barn tonight and he wants her to announce it on social media."

Buckner swiveled on her, fast.

"She's working for Delray?"

"No, no. She's working for the wolf. She's going to announce this fundraiser at the Barn tonight. She's going to do a social media thing and then come over here and talk to Meg Harper."

"Sky's going to come over here?"

"Yeah. She's going to announce drink specials at the Barn and free lappers, and that'll clear out these pricks. Then we can all go home. You heard Jewell and Delos are okay?"

"I heard that, yeah."

"It's been a day, huh?"

"And it ain't even close to being through, I'm afraid," said Buckner.

Foster Road cut through fields where the grass was tall and emerald green, and behind the fields were pinewoods and the east bank of the Crow River. Lucy could hear the river ramble south over its shallow sand-clay bottom, and the air was heavy and still and it smelled of mud and the sharp, rotten-egg undercurrent of hydrogen sulfide. There was standing water where the construction sediment had settled, and the gas stink was from the strangling vegetation.

The men across the road stood shoulder to shoulder and stared straight ahead and did not talk among themselves.

Buckner turned his head and spat.

"How long you think they worked on that little formation?"

"Standing in a line?" Lucy asked. "I bet it took them months, easy. Bless their hearts."

The militia were facing the sprawling, densely wooded Sawbrook acreage and according to the signs they'd placed on the road before them, they had come to demand they be granted passage onto the family property to search out the wolf they believed was roaming the hilltops above the river.

Meg Harper, the reporter, was standing outside the 9&10 News van with her camera crew. She wore a smart skirt and sleeveless blouse—had on hose and heels and stood with her back, Lucy noted, remarkably straight.

It was no secret that Meg Harper was a climber. She had designs on the network or a cable outlet—wanted nothing more than to be part of the endless churn of breaking stories and strong opinions and titillating chyrons. She did have a flair for the dramatic, too. Lucy knew because she read her blog.

There was nobody outside the 7&4 van. They were under the direction of Bill Sawton, who was playing out the string until retirement, and his people were soaking up the AC in the vehicle.

"Any idea when Sky's supposed to get here?" asked Buckner.

"I don't know. Maybe half an hour? Did you see Tom Brickett over there?"

"Is that Tom Brickett in the football helmet?"

"I believe so. And I believe that's his twin brother to his right. Toby."

"Makes me sick, Tom using official Cutler football apparel for this bullshit. Fucking Tom sucked. Dude never even played."

"D-Rod told me he saw their mother the other day and that she was as pleasant as she could be. Talking about how much she loves the park and uses our trails with her walking group. I guess she saw him at the grocery store in his uniform and came over just to say that. Then she told him that he might know her sons because they were around his age, but that sadly they'd taken after their father and weren't much good to the world."

"She said that? That they weren't much good to the world?"

"According to D-Rod that's exactly what she said."

Buckner adjusted his stance. Moved his weight from one foot to the other. "I would have bet anything those two didn't even have a mother. I always figured the Brickett boys were hatched out of an egg somewhere along the riverbank. And now you're telling me she's kind, and regularly exercises?"

"I know. It's one of those things that can't really be explained."

The Bricketts were twins, but not identical. Tom was not tall, maybe five foot nine, but he still had at least two inches on Toby. Tom was the skinny one and Toby was square shaped and carried himself in the aggressive, clipped manner of the little man with big things to prove.

It was Toby that began to motion in Lucy's direction.

She squinted across the road through her shades. There were heat ripples over the asphalt and she saw that Toby was waving a black handkerchief.

"Here we go," she said.

"Why's he waving that hanky?"

"I have no idea."

"Is he signaling for backup or something?"

"I think he just wants our attention."

"We're standing here, aren't we? What else does he want?"

Toby took a step forward, and she realized he was waving the handkerchief to alert the rest of the militia that he was breaking formation. Or at least that was what she assumed. There really was no way of knowing when it came to Sovereign North.

Now that he was clearly separated from the group, Toby shouted, "I'm about sick and tired of this bullshit!"

Lucy turned and looked behind her. Waited a moment.

"Are you talking to us?"

"You're damn right, I am!" he said. "You're the ones harboring a fucking wolf, aren't you?"

Buckner spoke to his sister beneath his breath.

"Please, let me punch this motherfucker."

"Definitely not worth it," she said. "I'm not looking to be a part of any gunfights this afternoon."

"You understand what I'm saying, though? It's so hot out here. I should be sitting on the porch right now with an iced tea."

"This is going to be their big move. They want to speak their piece and hope the news trucks film it. Let's walk out and meet them halfway. I don't want them standing over here in our shade."

Lucy and Buckner walked to the middle of the road, which stirred some commotion from Meg Harper and the 7&4 crew.

Toby took another step forward and the militia moved with him, in formation, two steps behind. The militia minus Arnold Givens, who Tom Brickett told to stay behind and stand guard.

"Guard what?" said Arnold.

"Our position."

"What's the difference?" Arnold said. "It's only about five feet."

"That's a precious five feet," said Tom.

"It's just gravel, dude. It's not like we're on the Arabian Peninsula."

Now Tom whipped around.

"Stay on that piece of dirt, Givens. There's a reason we have the ranks we do."

Lucy looked at Buckner, who looked back at her, wide-eyed.

"You think they can't be serious," she said. "But they are."

The militia now stood across the yellow center line from Buckner and Lucy. Up close, the men were pouring sweat and clearly tiring beneath the weight of their makeshift armor and gear.

"We know that wolf is up there," Tom said. "And you have no right to protect it."

"There's no wolf, Tom. And if there is, he's damn sure not on our property."

"Don't gaslight us, Lucy."

"Thing is," said Chuck Baker, "is that you got no say in how we do or do not respond to a threat of this level."

Chuck Baker was a tall, slender man in thick glasses and a camouflage bucket hat. He was standing behind the Brickett brothers and his tone was measured in comparison.

"Legally," he added.

"First off," Lucy said, "there is no threat. Second, if there was a threat, which there isn't, you would have no legal rights beyond those you are usually afforded."

"That wolf changes everything," Baker said. "My wife won't leave our bedroom she's so afraid."

"There's nothing for her to be afraid of, Chuck, is the thing."

"Just go on home, boys," said Buckner. "You've proved your point."

"Is that a threat?" said Toby.

"No," said Buckner. "It's just some advice."

Lucy looked up and down the line of men. The Bricketts were mouthy, but they both looked exhausted and so did the rest of their crew. They'd come to rattle their sabers and stir up some shit, but they were done now. This was the big standoff and what they really wanted was to find a cool room where they could drink cold beer.

The only man that appeared to be there for real, and this surprised her greatly, was Chuck Baker. Chuck was an accountant in town, and a decent enough man, but she'd heard his wife had been upset by the wolf and she had a history of depression. Of all the men standing across from her now, it was only Baker that she believed might actually try something.

She cleared her throat, then spoke calmly and not unkindly to the men.

"The thing is, if you really wanted to do something you wouldn't be standing here talking to us. You wouldn't have said a goddamn word to us about anything. You would have stormed onto our property, guns blazing. I'm glad you didn't do that, because there's no wolf to find, and if there was, you boys wouldn't have a chance in hell of actually getting to it. You'd have wasted the rest of your day over nothing, at best. At worst, you'd have gotten shot up and died."

"We have every right in the world to protect ourselves," said Chuck Baker.

"I believe that you believe that, Chuck," she said. "But what I'm telling you is true. Legally, for sure. But also psychologically. None of you boys really wants to go up in those hills because you know it's illegal and you know it's dangerous and a waste of time. Also, you're just too damn lazy."

"I don't have to stand here and listen to these insults," said Toby Brickett.

Buckner agreed.

"You sure don't. You're free to leave right this minute and go on home, Toby. Nobody is stopping you from that but yourself."

Lucy's voice was still calm, and almost understanding now.

"Look, I know you boys are all riled up right now, or at least you were before you had to stand there in the sun for two hours, but I also know that before too much longer you'll be packing up your shit to head home and you will be glad and greatly relieved to do so."

"We're not going anywhere," said Tom. "We're not giving an inch."

"That's right," Toby said.

"Amen," offered Chuck Baker.

Lucy did not recognize the man at the end of the line to her right. He was a ginger, tall and bearded, and she realized now that he was wearing a Colorado Avalanche hockey helmet.

"What about you, Forsberg?" she said. "You got anything to add, or you just going to stand there like some mystery on the mountain?"

"My name isn't Forsberg and I'm not saying a goddamn thing. I'm here in support and solidarity of my brothers."

Buckner must have just noticed the Avalanche helmet, too, because he shook his head in dismay at the rest of the group.

"You disgust me," he said. "Out here with a fucking Colorado Avalanche fan? Good Lord."

Out of everything the Sawbrooks said, this was the one thing for which the Sovereign North militia had no response.

After a moment, Toby waved his black handkerchief and turned to walk back to his side of the road. The rest of the men, in turn, put their backs to the siblings and prepared to follow him, but not before the Colorado fan nodded at Lucy.

"I'm impressed you know who Peter Forsberg is," he said. "I'll admit it."

"Of course I know who Peter fucking Forsberg is, he's a Hall of Famer, and you got a lot of nerve wearing an Avalanche helmet around here. More stupid than brave, I'm afraid."

"Either way," he said. "Respect."

"I don't want your respect. Or need it."

"And yet you have it, because it is a gift I have given freely."

"And yet I reject it," she said. "With extreme prejudice."

Toby Brickett yanked the man's arm, and he finally turned around and joined the rest of them as they returned to their spot on the bright side of the road.

Buckner and Lucy waited for the militia to cross, then made their way back to their shade.

"I can't believe the sheriff's department hasn't even sent a squad car," said Buckner.

"I told you they were in cahoots with the bad guys on this."

"I know, but it's one thing to hear it and another to see it in action."

Lucy checked her watch.

"Ten minutes and this will all be over."

"The wolf thing will be over?"

"No. This part of the wolf thing will be over."

A door slammed behind the 9&10 News van and now Bill Sawton was hurrying over to the Sawbrook side. Sawton was wearing a bright-pink bicycle helmet and an orange hunting jacket. He had no crew or cameras or microphones with him, and barely nodded at the Sawbrooks as he walked into the brush directly behind them.

Buckner gave Lucy a sideways glance and whispered, "What the hell is he doing?"

Sawton unzipped his pants and Buckner realized he'd walked all the way over to their area to take a piss so he could have their bodies between him and the militia while he did it. On the back of his jacket was a long piece of silver duct tape on which somebody had written JOURNALIST in felt marker.

Afterward, he zipped back up and only paused for a brief moment to tell the Sawbrooks that his wife, Ginny, had sent him with donuts that afternoon.

"We got some left in the van if you get hungry."

"All right," said Buckner. "Thank you."

"There's only apple fritters left, which she insists on buying for some reason. Everything else got gobbled right up."

Sawton hustled to the van and Buckner watched him until the rear door swung open and the reporter disappeared inside.

"Is that his wife's bike helmet, do you think? That was bright pink."

"No, that was from the breast cancer fundraiser the Jaycees put on. When everybody biked a mile to the beer tents down by the waterfront. He reported on it live and I remember he wore that helmet to raise awareness."

"I was just sitting here thinking Ginny Sawton must have an enormous head if her helmet fits on her husband like that."

"No," said Lucy. "Ginny's petite."

"Okay, well that makes more sense."

Now there was commotion near the 9&10 van. A sedan had driven into view and parked down the road, and Meg Harper was already moving toward it and barking out orders to her crew.

The car was an old-school Impala—maybe an '85—and it idled for a long few moments before the passenger door swung open.

"There she is," said Lucy.

Sky stepped out of the car in a short summer dress and heels. Her hair was down and curled at the ends where it fell over her shoulders, and even at a distance Buckner was floored.

"Good grief," he said.

"I don't understand it, Buckner."

"Understand what?"

"You and her. I'm not saying that to be mean, either. I mean, I actually don't get it. It is beyond the capacity of my mind to comprehend. Again, I mean that sincerely. It's a compliment, really."

"I completely agree," he said.

Meg Harper walked toward Sky, and the camera crew set up their shots while the militia broke formation to crane their necks and see.

"Can I ask you something, Buck?"

"I don't know, try it and see."

"How do you not live every day in fear that she's going to leave you?"

"That was something Harold helped me with, actually."

"How did Harold help you with that?"

"Harold loved her and he never would have loved a woman who was going to do me harm. He would have barked his little heart out if she wasn't right for me."

Lucy looked at her brother. It was so endearing and utterly enraging that his logic, which she found infantile and reductive, worked for him so entirely. It was her instinct to poke holes in his reasoning and there was a time she would have, but he was sober now and, like a pitcher in the late innings of a no-hitter, it was simply best not to say anything at all that could jeopardize the strange magic that seemed to be hovering above everything he touched these days.

"Why is Meg Harper interviewing her, though?" he asked. "Did Delray set that up?"

"He did. He texted her when he saw the news and said he was sending over a spokesperson to announce a community event."

"And she agreed to that?"

"Apparently, she owes him one. He helped her with some trouble she had with a resorter he knew from the Boogie Down."

"What kind of trouble?"

"I don't know, he didn't say."

Sky finished her interview, blew Buckner a kiss, and within moments telephones across the road began to ping and beep and vibrate. The men exchanged a flurry of glances and whispers, and then Toby Brickett signaled to break formation and decamp.

"They're headed to the Barn, aren't they?" Buckner said.

"Happy hour drink specials and then a raffle for free lappers," said Lucy. "So yeah, I'd say that's exactly where they're going."

the sawbrooks

They gathered that evening for dinner at Jewell's. They were all exhausted, and they knew the fight had just begun, but the mood was celebratory and relieved. The siblings watched Sky's interview twice while she changed into sweatpants and a T-shirt and started on dinner.

The boy was asleep in Jewell's room and she took Buckner and Lucy through what had happened the night before while Frog, back from Grandma's, bashed the living room floor with a mallet.

Jewell told about the stolen rifle, Delos's previous stint in Woodyard, and how he'd outrun her from the stoplight on Hiawatha Trail all the way to the Harbor North Resort. She recounted what happened on the boat, too. How he'd taken out two men with the same beer bottle when she had been unable to defend herself, and when Buckner pressed her for information on the men, Jewell waved him off.

"Don't make this about you and your anger. Not right now. We need to focus on the boy and the wolf. I'm not letting Delos spend another day in Woodyard, so if you want to do something to help me, think on that."

"We can not just let that go. They tried to—"

Buckner couldn't even say the word.

"We're going to let it go," Jewell said. "For now, that's exactly what we're going to do. This is not your call."

"She's right," said Lucy. "Right now it's the boy and it's the wolf. That's plenty on our plates. And I don't know what to do about Delos, because we can't just hide him here forever, and it sounds like he's going to Woodyard if we don't."

Frog hit the floor with the mallet and laughed. Buckner sighed.

"When do we get that fladry hung up?"

"First light tomorrow," said Lucy. "We're all going to get a good night's sleep, and we'll get up in the morning and get after it."

"And what's all this going on at the Barn tonight?"

"That's just Delray's thing. He's raising money and awareness. I'll link back up with him tomorrow."

There was music playing softly in the kitchen and Sky sang along while she cooked. They sat for a moment, all of them exhausted, but together.

After a time, Jewell turned to Lucy.

"You think all that stuff with the militia will get the MDR off its ass? You think they'll come out with a statement?"

"Nope. I don't think anything will get anybody off their ass short of video of the wolf itself, or maybe if he eats the wrong somebody's cat."

"That's pretty fucked up," Buckner said. "The way some cats' lives are prioritized over other cats. You got a barn cat dead and nobody cares, but kill one of Mrs. Jennings's cats and it'd be a five-alarm fire. It's just like with humans. Certain kinds you can get away with doing whatever you want to them, other kinds you can't so much as look at them sideways."

Jewell was having a beer before dinner, and she tipped the bottle in Lucy's direction.

"My question is, What happens if we do get more wolves that follow this one? You'll get the construction stops and all that, but the town isn't going anywhere. Everybody will still be all riled up and upset."

Lucy nodded.

"You want to know what the end game is? If these wolves do get here and make a home for themselves?"

"That's what I'm asking," Jewell said. "Yeah."

"The end game is that nothing happens. I mean, people will be up in arms for a while. They'll hold a few more town halls. Do some more Facebook posts. Then some trail camera will catch three or four wolves walking somewhere, minding their own business, and there'll be another panic and more threats. A few letters to the editor and some dopes will probably get together and form a fucking wolf patrol or some stupid shit like that. They'll drive the back roads with shiners and rifles and be ten times as likely to run themselves into a telephone pole as they will be to so much as spot a gray. People will start to bring in their cats at night, or maybe they won't. Maybe a cat gets picked off here and there, but nobody really cares, because by that point the person should have known better.

"Time will pass and nothing will happen because wolves don't want to hurt people unless people try to hurt them, and at the end of the day we'll all manage the same way we do with bobcats and coyotes and black bears. The end game is that nothing happens, because it is in our nature, despite what they think down at the town hall, to get along just fine. And in the very, very unlikely case that the wolf population gets too big, they'll issue a few hunting licenses and turn it into tourism."

"So people will just get used to it?" Buckner asked.

"Most people will get used to it because most people will get bored and need something new to worry over when this doesn't pan out to be the end of the world."

"That actually makes sense," Buckner said.

Jewel nodded her agreement.

"No shit it makes sense," said Lucy. "That's why it's the plan."

Sky called everybody for dinner just after five. A little early, but they were going to load up on pasta and sleep right after. Sky had made her red sauce with sausage and Sawbrook tomatoes and it was tangy and sweet and they ate it over spaghetti at the big table in the dining room. There was garlic bread and a salad that Lucy had gathered from the garden, and Delos had woken up from a dead sleep, then sat down at the table and inhaled his first plate before anybody, even Buckner, was halfway through with their own.

"Go on then," said Sky, and scooped him a second helping from the serving bowl.

Buckner pointed at Lucy.

"You know what I was thinking?"

"I can only imagine."

"This whole plan, turning the property into a makeshift preserve, going against the MDR, it's almost like Rhoda came up with it herself. That's how crazy it is."

"It's not that crazy," said Lucy.

"The hell it isn't," said Jewell. "This whole thing is more Rhoda than Rhoda herself. All the lying and conniving? I didn't know you had it in you."

"It's the right thing to do," Lucy said. "It's no more complicated than that."

"That's all well and good," Jewell answered. "But it still has Mom all over it. You know it's true. Isn't it, Buck?"

"It is to me," he said. "I'm the one that said the comparison first."

Lucy looked down at her mostly gone spaghetti. She could have dropped it, knew she should drop it, but it just wasn't accurate.

"Rhoda might like the plan, but she never would have thought of it."

Jewell was drinking a second beer with dinner, and she looked at Lucy over her bottle of Budweiser.

"What does that mean?"

"Are you saying you're smarter than Mom?" said Buckner. "'Cause that's where I draw the line."

"I didn't say I was smarter. I just said she wouldn't have thought of it."

Jewell scoffed.

"How's that any different?"

"It's completely different. Every single one of Mom's plans was about keeping this land in our possession. This plan doesn't have anything to do with us. All this does is put a target on our backs. We're doing it 'cause it's the right thing."

"You're also doing it to shut down construction."

"It's a nice aside, but that's not the reason."

"Just take the compliment, Luce," said Buckner.

"I don't really consider it a compliment, or think it's accurate."

"Jesus God," Jewell said. "You try and say something halfway nice and it blows up in your face."

Buckner scooped some more spaghetti onto his plate, then looked at Lucy across the table.

"Jewell's right. It's a great plan, Lucy, but that doesn't mean you get to be a dick about it."

Lucy pushed her chair back from the table.

"Oh, for God's sake. I'm going to bed. You two can just sit here and babble at each other."

Lucy stood up and Sky seized the serving bowl from Buckner and offered it to Delos. The boy nodded and she doled him out more spaghetti and red sauce and rolled her eyes at the siblings. The boy gave her a little smile.

"Hold on, Luce," said Buckner.

"What is it now?"

He held up his hand, but it wasn't to argue another point.

"Do you hear that?"

The table grew quiet, but Delos was still tearing into his thirds. He slurped a long noodle and then Sky put a hand on his forearm and he looked up from his plate and stopped chewing. Outside, they heard a yipping sound.

"Turn off the radio!" Lucy shouted.

Sky was closest, and she jumped up from the table and cut the power to the Bluetooth speaker in the kitchen. Now the yipping grew louder and more distinct.

"Is that the wolf?" asked Jewell.

"I don't know," said Buckner.

Lucy shook her head.

"That's not the wolf," she said. "No way."

The sound was high-pitched and squeaky, more puppy than anything else. Specifically, it sounded like a puppy in some sort of pain, and Buckner shoved himself away from the table and ran for the door. Sky shouted his name but he was already gone. Frog started crying in his bassinet and Delos looked at Jewell and his eyes were like blue-gray saucers.

"That's not him."

"What?" said Jewell.

"That's not him."

The boy had never heard the wolf cry, but it was far too thin and small of a sound. He knew for certain it wasn't him.

Outside, leaves rattled and there was a series of snapping branches and then a *whooosh* sound, like a tunnel of wind, and Sky was still shouting for Buckner, and when the rest of the table turned to face the big front window, they all saw the wolf—its fur black in the light and its strides strong and smooth. They could see the torsion of its big shoulders and how fluid and powerful the sum of the motion was—how purposeful and arrow straight.

The wolf cleared their view in one gallop and now Buckner was running behind it and Delos darted for the door and Jewell lunged and grabbed him by the shirt and they both fell to the floor. The boy wriggled free and when she tried to grasp him a second time her hand only swiped at the open space he'd left behind him.

the wolf

The wolf dispersed from its pack in the deep of winter, when the snow had piled for nearly seven weeks in the pines of the Hiawatha Forest and the pack was hungry but not yet thinning.

The wolf was full-grown and needed food but there was something in his heart that propelled him into the dark forest, and when the pack brayed behind him he did not feel pulled to return but only pushed himself farther away from the one land he had ever known.

The wolf ate well beyond the reach of the pack and moved quickly on his own. He would bed down in the snow and sleep and it was colder at night without the body heat of the pack but he pushed still farther and ran through the pines with the snow falling gently, and everything was white and emerald green and untouched.

The wolf called for others, but not the ones he had left behind. There was no answer, and so he ran farther and faster, and before long he was outside of the forest and it was colder in the wind with no cover from the trees, and the slope of the land was unfamiliar. There were open spaces and strange lights in the distance and his calls became more urgent, and when they were not returned, he would feel flutters of fright and desperation, and sometimes he would bed down for the night in the snow and whimper.

Finally, he came to the shores of Lake Huron and he stepped out onto the ice. It was solid beneath him and he crossed at night with the sky black and cloudless and the stars bright and spread above him.

On the ice there was an absence of smell and of movement and shape, and the wolf trotted a straight line through that empty world between shores, and when he reached the other side he began to climb into the hills where there were trees and long stretches of rock and damp caves where he would find water and drink and rest.

He brayed at night and moved around the hills, and the quiet that returned to him began to burrow into his heart and become heavy, but he did not stop searching and he did not stop calling.

In the spring the snow began to melt and run for the low ground in rivulets that gleamed in the sun and he would drink from those streams and hunt the small animals. He was not hungry anymore, but he was not done searching, either. He pushed west now, toward the light that bled out a little longer with each passing day.

The summer came and he found a cave in the sandstone hills where there was small game to hunt and the bushes were heavy with berries, and food that he did not kill was delivered to him on the sides of roads. Once, a woman brought him meat and he felt no fear or sadness when she was close, but she was not what he called out for or needed.

He was asleep in his narrow cave the night the pup cried, and as soon as he heard the sound he woke and ran toward it, and for the first time since he dispersed he felt pulled toward another wolf. He charged hard through the trees because he knew the pup was in danger, and the gray's heart and the totality of his existence was only concerned in that moment with this young one that he already loved and would die to protect.

There was no space in the gray's heart for doubt or even a sense of his own bravery and valor. There was nothing in the wolf at all but his roaring love and the hard muscles of his legs and his speed, and he returned the pup's call and burst into a clearing where he smelled the poacher but he did not understand what the smell was or the danger he was in.

The poacher was just something between him and the pup, and he charged at the scent and the shape in the dark, and when the first bullet was fired and missed he felt the burst of the air and heard the *whoosh* and for just one moment his senses were lost and scrambled and he was alone in the clearing without his every resource and mechanism for survival. The sound of the second shot was nearer than the first, and when the bullet struck his head the wolf only saw a line in the distance where everything went flat and white—a stretch of uncut snow between the pines of the forest like the very one where he'd been reared.

Then he fell into the snow and he was gone, and so was the unrequited courage of his good and noble heart.

part IV

the sawbrooks

Jewell was on the run for the clearing when she heard the first shot—the short crack of it—and the second that came right after. The percussive thunder of the wolf's charge stopped all at once, and then came the terrible thud when its body hit the ground.

The night went still and she heard the crickets hum in the brush and felt a gust of wind that blew through the high top of the canopy.

Buckner was down in the field about ten yards behind the wolf and he was groaning, and it was too dark to see the blood but she could tell he was badly injured. Delos was on his hands and knees, and the poacher was above the dead wolf. She shouted for help and leaned over Delos and put her hand on the small of his back.

She heard zippers open and close, sudden and sharp, and the poacher grunting with effort, and she turned and saw her brother with one hand on his wounded shoulder. He was trying to stand. She shouted again for help and when Delos tried to run at the poacher she gathered him in her arms.

A truck roared to life up the hill and the high beams cut the night through the trees and she could see the dark bloom of blood on her brother's upper body and the swirl of insects that whirred in the light shafts between the pines, and everything was flickering and brightly fractured.

Lucy was barreling down the hill in her pickup, and Jewell thought her sister would arrive just in time to catch the poacher, but then there was a blast of sound and the headlights went sideways and everything in the field returned to black and there was a boom that shook the ground beneath her as Lucy careened into the pine trees.

The poacher had hoisted the wolf on his back and he was laboring for the tree line at the edge of the clearing. Sky was with Buckner now and Jewell could hear him shouting that the poacher was Darnette Lewis.

"It's Darnette! I know it for a fact!"

The boy tried to escape her grip, but Jewell held on and he did not escape her. He was shouting and sobbing and his thin voice crackled, then broke, and it was the most terrible sound that she had ever heard.

Lucy knew immediately that her shoulder was dislocated, but the far greater concern was the engine fire and the pine trees around it that were set to go off like rockets if the flames reached the crowns. Especially with how dry it had been all summer.

The truck was pinned between two trees, with the driver's side nearest to the ground. The airbags had both deployed, and when she unclipped her belt she dropped against the door and landed squarely on her already injured shoulder. She gritted her teeth and grunted.

Rhoda had always had her issues with Lucy, but she was the toughest of the siblings and that was something her mother had openly admired. It didn't make anything hurt any less, but Lucy did feel a sense of obligation to get herself up and get the fire dealt with, because whatever hurt now was nothing compared to the agony and embarrassment of being the park ranger that couldn't stop her own damn forest from burning.

The center console was flipped open and she snapped the window breaker out of the storage clip on the inside of the lid. The breaker was a small red tube with a neon-yellow stripe so she could see it in the dark, though the engine fire was growing and helping with that cause. She unscrewed the top of the breaker, put the spring-loaded cylinder to the glass behind her, heard the click and then the shatter.

The glass was tempered, of course, and she was able to push it out in large chunks with her hand, then she kicked with her legs and forced herself through the open window and she was standing outside of the truck.

She ran up the hill to the family's old taxidermy shed, pushed the door open, and took a fire extinguisher off the wall. She ran back with the extinguisher cradled in one arm and her other arm dangling loosely at her side, and each step she took sent a reverberation of eye-peeling pain that ran on a rope directly into the soft tissue of her exposed shoulder.

She came up close to the fire so she could put her foot against the truck and balance the extinguisher on her leg as she pulled the pin and finally shot the foam at the flames and buried them in the dry chemical discharge.

Moments later, Jewell watched in horror when Lucy came staggering into the clearing with her left arm dangling low at her side.

"It's out," Lucy said, flatly. "My shoulder is out. That fucker put down spikes. The truck is totaled."

"I'll get my truck," Jewell said. "We'll get everybody to the ER."

"Check for spike strips. From here up."

"What do they look like?"

"It's a strip with fucking spikes on it. That's what it looks like. He put one down by the house and there might be more. Just check the road. Flip on your phone light and look."

Jewell did find another strip, right near the clearing, and she pulled it off the road and tossed it into the brush. She jogged, but scanned the road as she took a mental inventory of the total damage in the field.

The wolf was dead. Buckner was shot. Lucy had dislocated her shoulder, and the boy, she believed, had been struck once and knocked to the ground. She would drive to the hospital with Sky in back with the wounded. She would call Connie to come up and watch Frog and Delos.

She reached the top of the hill, climbed into the pickup, and drove very slowly, peering out over the wheel at the road until she reached the clearing, put the truck in park, and popped the tailgate.

She ran to Sky first, to help with Buckner.

Her brother was bleeding badly. There were big, sticky washes of blood down his side and stomach and he was struggling with each step. He was cursing beneath his breath at Darnette, and then he apologized to both Jewell and Sky for getting shot.

"I'm sorry you all got to deal with this right now. Goddamnit, he got away."

Lucy was in the driver's seat of Jewell's truck and shouted for them to hurry.

"He's losing blood!"

"You're not driving!" shouted Jewell. "Your shoulder."

"I don't need two shoulders to drive. Stay in the back with Buckner and do what you can to stop the blood."

Jewell shouted right back.

"Do not try to be a hero right now, Lucy! Let me drive!"

"I'm not trying to be a hero! I'm trying to drive the goddamn truck. Get in and help our brother, goddamnit!"

Lucy revved the engine and that was the end of the argument. Sky and Jewell each took one side of Buckner's body and set their legs behind them and pushed him into the back of the pickup and he screamed out as he fell forward and landed. Sky scrambled up behind him and then Jewell hopped in and pulled up the tailgate and they were flying down the hill.

Buckner turned to his wife and whispered that he loved her.

"I love you, too," she said. "But if you die, I swear to God I'm going to kill you."

delos

I can't really remember exactly what happened after Darnette smacked me in the head. I knew the wolf was dead and I remember screaming and blood and I remember hearing a sound like a bomb going off back up toward Jewell's house.

I see it all in flashes. I can recall little bits and pieces, but nothing is strung together in a way where I could tell what happened when, and there are parts that are pure empty between what I remember, but I figure that I must have walked up to Jewell's house after they went to the hospital because when my memory kicks in and gets clear I'm sitting in Buckner and Sky's trailer with Jewell's pistol in my hand and baby Frog asleep in the bassinet beside me.

I knew that Connie was coming to watch me and Frog. I remember somebody shouting about that, but I wasn't going to be there when she arrived. I couldn't leave Frog alone, but the moment that Connie got there I was going to cut out the back door and run straight for Darnette Lewis's place.

I knew exactly where he lived, too. The Jessups were on Henderson Road just a quarter mile from his place. They were the religious ones, and Mrs. Jessup always used to warn us about Darnette—almost as much as she went on about drugs and sex and false idols and being gay. She said to never let him in the door.

"I don't care if his hair is on fire," she'd said. "You keep the locks closed and let him burn."

I was angry sitting on that couch in the trailer, but not out of control. I had felt out of control at first, right after Darnette hit me. Right after I realized the wolf was gone, I'd been crying and shouting and all those sounds and all that hurt were coming out of me and even if I had wanted, there was nothing I could do to tamp it back. It had all spilled out in a big, ugly stew, but that part was over now. Now I'd moved myself into a different way of feeling about things. I'd gone numb, but I was thinking clearly. I was going to kill Darnette Lewis.

It wasn't long before I saw the headlights in the dark and heard the car climbing the hill. Then I heard a door slam and a woman's voice and I knew that it was Connie. I could see her walking toward the trailer behind a little beam from a flashlight, and I lit out of the back door and I ran.

The hardest part of the run was the first few miles through the forest between the Sawbrooks' houses and the river. I didn't know exactly where I was going, but I knew that if I kept moving down then eventually I would hit the river and I could follow the Crow almost all the way to Darnette's.

I didn't hear the crickets or the tree frogs as I ran. The only sound in my ears was a white hum, like a big fan whirring in an empty warehouse, and my legs didn't tire and I could not feel my feet pounding the dirt or scuffing the tops of the tree roots because I took each step on pure adrenaline and hate.

There was light along the water when I got to the river, but I didn't take cover in the tree line. I ran along the bank because it was faster in the open and I passed the quiet, empty fairways and the big houses that were built back off the water, and then I passed the falls and did not even hear the water dropping. I made it to Crooked Tree Park and cut toward the intersection of Hiawatha Trail and Henderson.

I had always been fast and could always run distance, but I don't think I'd ever run so far so quickly—not even when I was trying to get away from Jewell—and I was not tired at all.

If anything, I felt stronger in my legs than when I'd started back at the property, and I believe I could have run forever that night if that was what was needed.

I saw the wolf drop and how everything left its body all at once. How quickly its life was taken, and how completely. There was no struggle or drama to it at all. The bullet hit the wolf and dropped him and it was like a door slamming closed. He was dead.

I hit Henderson Road and I was close now. I had not seen a single car or person out in the night, though it probably wouldn't have mattered if I had. I was not going to stop, not for anything.

Henderson Road was surrounded by marsh and everything there smelled like sulfur. That is the one thing that cut through my anger—that rotten-egg stink.

There used to be wildflowers. Mrs. Jessup would point out the blooms and call them by name. I remember she said they were blazing star and pitcher's thistle and I had thought those names and those flowers were pretty, but now there was nothing but standing water and insects and the burnt smell that worked its way deep into my nostrils and damn near made my eyes water.

Finally, I saw the opening where Darnette's drive met the road and I did not pause there or stop to gather myself and I was not afraid or unclear about why I was there. I knew exactly what was going to happen.

jewell

Jewell sat with Sky in the waiting area outside of surgery. The Cutler hospital was old and dimly lit and smelled of bleach and isopropyl alcohol and sadness and fear. Cutler people liked to joke that the hospital was the leading cause of death, and while that may have been hyperbole there was also no way to sit in that lobby and feel confident that the best possible care, or even adequate care, was being provided to a loved one.

Buckner was not going to die, though. Jewell was nearly certain of that. He had taken a shot in the shoulder, and he had lost a lot of blood, but he was young and strong and he wanted to live.

Sky was less certain.

"He bled so much, and this place fucking sucks. They kill healthy people here, let alone ones with holes in their shoulders."

There was an older woman in the lobby with them. She was watching the television—a home renovation show—and shot Sky a look. Sky shot the look right back.

"What? You disagree."

"I disagree with your language, young lady."

"Well, I disagree with you giving a fuck about my language when my husband is in there with his shoulder all blasted to pieces."

The woman's mouth dropped open and Sky stared at her and did not grant her the relief of glancing away. The woman had on a gray sweatsuit. Her white hair was short and curly and she wore thick, red-framed glasses. Finally, the woman stood down and returned her gaze to the television.

Jewell put her hand on Sky's back and held it there. She tried to be strong for her, though she did not know, specifically, what strength in that situation entailed.

"As long as he lives," Sky said, "I can deal with anything else."

"He's going to live."

Sky seemed to try and accept this logic but couldn't quite get there. She chewed on her bottom lip and stared off into the room.

"I did not like that fuzzy-eyed doctor that wheeled him into surgery. He looked like he needed surgery just to stay awake. This crew might get half done and take a break for coffee and forget what they were doing in the first place. We don't get the All-Stars up here, Jewell, you know that. This is the minor leagues. Single-A ball."

Jewell ran her hand in circles around Sky's back. After a time, Sky turned to Jewell. Her eyes were red and bleary with tears.

"Why did he run toward it?"

"I don't know."

"What kind of man chases a fucking wolf?"

"I think he thought it might have been a pup."

"And what kind of fucking scumbag uses the sound of a frightened puppy to lure a wolf into a field and kill it?"

"I don't know. It's the money in the end. I think that's all it is."

Lucy was in the ER, and Jewell was going to go check on her shortly, but it was a dislocated shoulder and they would pop it back in, then give her some painkillers and a sling. The police would come, but Lucy had already told them they wouldn't do anything when it came to Darnette.

Sky was sitting up straight in her chair. She spoke to Jewell, but stared away into the lobby.

"We never talked much about this, but I loved your mom. I mean, I obviously didn't know her long, but I knew who she was and I respected her so much even before we met. But then in person she was even better. She was just so strong and smart. I wish I would have met your daddy, too."

Now Jewell was beginning to get teary.

"My daddy was sweet. They were a little bit of yin and yang."

"I want to take his name," Sky said. "Your name. I want to be a Sawbrook, if that's okay with you all."

"Of course it's okay."

Sky nodded toward the double doors that led into the ER.

"Even if he doesn't come out of there."

"He's coming out."

"Well, even so."

"You're already as much a Sawbrook as any of us," she said. "I mean, you married Buckner, plus the fact that you're crazy enough to want to be a Sawbrook is about the most qualifying thing in the world."

Sky waved the comment off.

"You're not that bad."

"Oh yes, we are," said Jewell. "We're that bad, and worse."

Jewell's phone rang. She checked the ID, saw it was Connie, and stood up to take the call. She could hear Connie breathing hard on the other end.

"The boy is gone."

"What?"

"The kid is gone. Delos."

"What do you mean, gone?"

"He's not here. I checked all three houses."

"Is Frog there?"

"He's asleep in the bassinet."

"He didn't leave a note or anything?"

"Not that I saw."

"You don't think he went to—"

"Jewell, I don't have any idea where that child went. But I will say this: I think it's safe to assume the worst. It's always the worst with you guys. So just think of the worst place he could possibly go, and then go there, and that's where he'll probably be."

Jewell hung up. Connie was right, of course. The boy had probably taken off running for Darnette Lewis's, assuming he knew where he lived, and while they hadn't been gone but an hour she knew better than to doubt the boy's capacity as a runner. She looked at Sky.

"Delos is gone."

"Oh, shit."

"I have to go get him."

Sky stood up and began to dig through her purse. She pulled out her pocket pistol, a little .22 she kept handy in case of emergency, and handed it to Jewell.

"How'd you get this through security?"

"I used to give lappers to Claude, who's running the machine."

Jewell nodded.

"Go!" shouted Sky.

delos

I was in front of Darnette's house when I heard the sound of the shovel, the scrape it made when the edges hit the hard ground, and I could hear Darnette breathing heavy and cursing between lifts. His yard was stony and scattered with weedy grass and I crouched low to the ground and moved slow as I worked my way around to the back.

I can't explain how or why everything was so clear all of the sudden, why I could hear and see it all when for the entire run over it was like I was trapped inside of myself and everything around me was in the black and pure quiet. Maybe it was the sulfur smell that cleared my senses, or maybe it was that I'd clicked off the safety on the gun in my hand.

I have learned that the distance between Buckner's house and Darnette's is over four miles and I made that trip in less than forty minutes through rough terrain, but in my mind there are only two parts. There's the running part, when everything was fuzzy and dull, and then there's the part where everything kicks into full color and I see every detail and hear every sound.

The only thing I smell, though, is the sulfur. Sometimes I still smell it. I can be inside surrounded by four walls and that smell will sit down high in my nostrils and I will be back there in Darnette's yard all over again.

He didn't notice me right off. He was focused on the ground beneath him and I could see the lines on his face and how frustrated he was by the work, and I remember realizing that he was not upset at all by the wolf being dead, but by the fact that he had to labor so hard to bury it.

There were dirt piles around Darnette, and the wolf was on its side and I could not see the color of the blood in the dark but I could see the places where the fur clumped together. His paws were dangling loose and his mouth was slightly open and his ears looked softer and smaller somehow. I was beyond the cover of the house and in the open space and I lifted my gun and put it on Darnette, and it was not at all heavy in my hand.

Darnette still didn't notice me. He just kept jabbing his shovel and cursing and tossing dirt.

I was between him and the wolf, and the wolf's eyes were open but they were empty, and I will never forget how flat they looked and how all the brightness had been taken away and how it happened so suddenly and how I knew it could not be changed. Not ever.

Darnette finally noticed me, or maybe he noticed my gun, and he stopped working and looked up from the shallow ditch.

"What the fuck?"

He took a step toward me but I straightened my arm and held the gun steady. Darnette glanced over my shoulder to where his rifle was lying in the grass near the house. I stood between him and his weapon and did not move.

"Who the fuck are you?"

I didn't answer. I did not say a word to Darnette. I did not warn him not to move or tell him to put his hands up or curse him for the terrible thing he had done. Instead, I set my feet firm beneath me and held my aim.

He waited for a few moments, then stepped out of the hole and walked right at me. He was going for his rifle and he did not believe that I would shoot him, not standing right there in the open yard. Not so close that I could see the lines on his face.

There was no fear at all in his eyes. He only looked angry and aggravated, put out by the fact that I had shown up with a gun and interrupted his task. I kept the pistol trained on his chest and I told myself to fire. I don't know if I said it out loud, or only thought it, but I said it to myself clearly—*shoot*.

I heard the clap of the gunshot and Darnette fell to the ground and I stood with my aim held and there was blood pouring down Darnette's leg and he was shouting in pain, and then I heard my name and I turned and saw Jewell walking toward me with the pistol that had shot Darnette.

"I need you to lower that," she said, and reached toward me.

I did lower my gun. I lowered it, then I felt my knees wobble and I dropped to the ground in pure exhaustion.

jewell

They could hear the sirens gathering in the distance. Jewell stood above Darnette while he cursed her, and Delos had moved to be beside the wolf, and the lights began to flicker red-blue through the treetops.

"You tried to kill me," he said.

"If I'd tried to kill you, you'd be dead. I put one in your hip with a .22. Calm down."

"Sheriff Dunn won't do shit to me," said Darnette. "This is all going to be for nothing, you know that, right?"

"At least I got to shoot you," said Jewell. "So no, not all for nothing."

The sheriff arrived first and parked on the side of the house and muted his sirens. He made his slow way toward the scene as two deputies in squad cars piled in behind him.

"I need an ambulance!" Darnette shouted.

"I told them to send one when I called this in," said Jewell. "Quit being so dramatic."

Darnette groaned. Struggled to lift his head to see the sheriff approaching.

"Look how fucking slow that man moves. That damn waddle is going to get somebody killed someday. Hopefully him."

Jewell did not look at the sheriff or Darnette. Jewell stared off at a line of trees in the distance.

"I really just wish you'd lay there and bleed and not be so loud about it."

"If I don't bleed out it's not for lack of trying, I'll tell you that."

"I shot you with a purse pistol, dude. You bleed to death out of your hip, it'd be a medical miracle for which we would all give thanks."

Finally, the sheriff arrived, flipped on his flashlight, and took in the surroundings.

"Jesus, Mary, and Joseph," he said. "You all right, Darnette?"

"No, I'm not all right, goddamnit! She shot me."

"I can see that. Ambulance is on its way right behind me."

The sheriff scanned the yard again. The dead wolf and the shallow, unfilled grave. Jewell above Darnette, with the gun used to shoot the man still in her hands. An upset boy with the wolf. The pale stars above it all.

"Well, we got quite the little clusterfuck here, don't we?"

"It's a developing situation," said Jewell.

"I'm wondering what you have in mind, Jewell, since you called me and didn't hightail it out of here."

"I know you're not going to prosecute this piece of shit lying here in the dirt. I suspect he'll claim coyote, and since you are part of this whole operation you won't have much desire to see it go any further than that. I'm assuming the prosecutor won't give a shit, either."

"Do you know Jack?"

"I know enough to know he won't care about this. Might even get a cut on the side from the same folks you are."

"Anyway," said the sheriff. "Unfounded accusations aside, I agree with your assessment that charges are unlikely to be filed on this wolf."

"Thing is, though, he put a bullet right in my brother's shoulder in the process. Buckner is down at the ER right now. That happened on our property. Where he shot the wolf."

"Yeah, that's not good," said Sheriff Dunn.

"You're going to arrest her, aren't you?" said Darnette. "She fucking walked right into my backyard and shot me in the leg. Right after that crazy little bastard with the wolf materialized out of the goddamn ether and held me at gunpoint."

The sheriff ignored Darnette and turned to Jewell.

"We got about another minute here before everybody and their brother shows up. You want to tell me what you're thinking, or not?"

"I want to bury the wolf on our land. Obviously, you're not pressing charges on me because I'll just start telling everybody everything I know."

The sheriff nodded at Darnette on the ground.

"And what do we do with this mess?"

"He shot himself is what happened."

"The hell I did!"

The sheriff looked down at his own hip. Formed a gun with his thumb and pointer finger and then dropped his thumb like it was the hammer. He looked up at Jewell.

"That could maybe work."

"Self-inflicted wounds are very common when dealing with imbeciles and degenerates," Jewell said.

"No way," said Darnette. "Absolutely not."

The sheriff shot a look at Darnette on the ground.

"You want to get paid or don't you?"

"I'm getting paid, that's the one thing I do know—"

"Shut the fuck up, Darnette," snapped Dunn. "If she blows this up, then you don't get a red cent and you might actually do some prison time. So just sit there and be quiet for two seconds and let me see if I can't get your stupid ass out of this mess."

Dunn stepped away from Darnette and motioned Jewell over. She clicked the safety on the little .22 and slipped it in the back of her jeans.

"You can't put that wolf in the media," Dunn whispered. "You know that, right?"

"I won't put it in the media."

"And why would I believe you about that?"

Jewell looked at the boy. He was lying with his head on the wolf's belly and staring straight ahead.

"Because you're going to do something else for me to make all this even."

part V

delos

I couldn't believe that the sheriff let both me and Jewell walk away from Darnette's, but that's exactly what happened. He had a few of the deputies carry the wolf over and drop him into the back of Jewell's pickup, we covered his body with a tarp, and we passed the ambulance headed for Darnette's on our way back to the property.

Sky called from the hospital that night to let us know that Buckner was okay, and she drove Lucy home while Buckner stayed overnight. In the morning, me and Jewell dug a hole in the clearing where the wolf and Buckner had been shot and we buried him there.

"We'll get a little headstone for him," she said. "We'll mark the grave so we can remember him."

"Yes, ma'am."

"I told you to quit calling me ma'am."

"I know. I'm sorry. I'm tired and I just forgot."

"It's all right. Go get showered up. We're going to drive you over to the Bakers."

"I don't want to go back there."

"You're not going back there. You and me are going to pay

him for the rifle you stole, and you're going to apologize to him for taking it."

"They're going to take me back to county then."

"No, they're not."

"How do you know?"

"Because I settled it with Dunn. That's what we were talking about right before we left Darnette's. You're with us now. You're staying right here, if that's okay with you."

"Are you serious?"

She nodded.

"It's not official yet, but it's what's going to happen."

I hugged her right then. I wanted her to know how happy I was before she had a chance to change her mind, and I did not want to let go, either. I just wrapped my arms around her and held on.

Jewell was going to pay Mr. Baker cash for the rifle but told me I would have to work off the debt.

"And you can't steal my own money out of my own wall, like you did my gun last night."

I shook my head.

"I'm sorry about that. I really am."

"We'll talk about that later. We'll set up some real clear guidelines that include you not running off with anything that isn't yours. Buckner will want you to play football, but you can get a job and work on the weekend to pay me back."

Mr. Baker was sitting out on the porch when we arrived. I was glad to see there weren't empty beer cans scattered everywhere like there had been when I left. He was drinking an iced tea and he offered us both something to drink and that was good because I was worried he was going to greet me with a list of accusations and complaints.

I was thirsty but I told him I was fine. My mouth was all dry from being nervous, but I didn't want to put him out, not after Jewell said she didn't need anything.

I told him I was sorry, and in a way, I was. I wasn't sorry that I'd taken the rifle to try and protect the wolf, but I was sorry that I'd had to steal it from him to do it.

"You were real good to me and I apologize for what I did," I said. "You didn't deserve that."

Mr. Baker nodded. He said it took a man to face down his own mistakes and that he accepted my apology. I was hoping that Mrs. Baker would be better, but she was not downstairs and Mr. Baker didn't say much about her. We were just there a few minutes and afterwards he stood up and shook my hand and then shook Jewell's hand and told me that he'd be rooting for me in life and that he believed I would make something of myself if I could just stay out of trouble.

Jewell thanked him for not pressing charges, and then I said I was sorry again and when we turned to leave I looked up at Mrs. Baker's bedroom window and she was standing there in a nightgown looking down at us and she put her palm flat against the glass.

We had two meetings with Ms. Mary in one week and it was mostly her helping Jewell fill out forms. Every once in a while she'd say that she needed to speak with Jewell in private and I'd go out into the main lobby and flip through magazines.

Jewell said we were going to have to see the judge, but that Ms. Mary had made sure everything was in order and that I would be turned over to Jewell's custody within a matter of weeks.

"You're going to be my foster parent?"

"I'm going to be your mom, dude. But yeah, at first it'll be temporary custody until all the paperwork gets sorted."

"My mom? For real?"

"One thing about being a Sawbrook," she said, "is we don't do anything half-ass. I'm going to take care of you and you're going to live on the property and Lucy and Buckner and Sky will be your aunts and uncle, and Frog will be your cousin. And I'll leave this part up to you, but I'd like to go ahead and change your last name to Sawbrook."

We were driving home from Ms. Mary's. We were going through town and I remember seeing the sun above the buildings in the shopping district, and the sky stretched out was bright blue and there were no clouds and I knew that I would never be happier in a single moment for the rest of my life than I was right then. I was too shocked to make a sound, but I had tears streaming down my cheeks and I couldn't have stopped them if I'd tried.

the sawbrooks

The night Jewell received full custody of Delos, the first step in the process of his adoption, the adults celebrated with a bonfire. The boys were in bed and Jewell and Sky had stacked a pallet on the firepit while Lucy and Buckner sat in their lawn chairs with their shoulder injuries.

Jewell said she wanted to take Delos school shopping at the mall in Traverse City, and Buckner said she needed to hurry up and get it done before football started.

"Two-a-days are coming up," he said. "And I already talked to Coach Benton about Delos. He thinks he's got enough wide receivers and that Delos is going to be third string, maybe play some special teams, but that'll be out the window by the end of the first practice. We got an all-conference flanker in the family, maybe all-state."

"Flanker?" said Lucy. "What is this, 1970?"

"Whatever they call them now," said Buckner. "That's what that boy is."

Jewell said she had some information on Delos, that she'd gone to the court and pulled a file on his mother.

"I looked that up," said Lucy. "Don't you need birth certificates to get all that stuff?"

"Not when the clerk is Patricia Danning."

"I thought she moved to Colorado," Buckner said.

"She's back now. Working for the county. We were buddies in high school so she let me snap some pictures with the phone."

Lucy leaned toward her sister.

"And?"

"And Delos's mother, our cousin, was left at Sisters of the Redemptive Light as a newborn. The old nun orphanage. The birth certificate is from San Diego, where Uncle William was stationed, but he's not listed as the father."

"Then how do you know she was our cousin? We haven't got the DNA back yet."

"Because there was a note."

"What kind of note?"

Jewell clicked her phone on and passed it to Lucy.

"This kind."

Lucy looked at the screen. There was an old piece of notebook paper with frayed, yellowing edges, and she zoomed in and read aloud what was written.

> This baby is called Delores Johnson, but you can change her name if you like. Her father is William Sawbrook but he was killed in the Army while I was pregnant. I cannot keep her alone and William's family will not have us. They will not even see us. I loved him and I am sorry.

Buckner waited for his sister to continue, but she was done. She passed the phone back to Jewell and shook her head.

"I cannot believe Grandma did that. It's unforgivable. That was our cousin."

"Makes me sick," said Buckner.

"Do you think Mom knew?" asked Jewell.

"God, I hope not," said Lucy.

"No way," said Sky. "She didn't know or she would have done something about it. For sure."

The siblings turned to Buckner's wife. At first, they were surprised that Sky had weighed in on the subject of their mother, but she had spoken directly and without apology, and because she had known Rhoda so briefly it also granted her a strange bit of authority—her judgment was unclouded by history and the catalog of both favorable memories and personal grievances that each of the siblings brought to all discussions involving their mother.

She was right, of course. Rhoda would have done something if she'd known. The one thing about their mother that was beyond dispute was that she would always, for better or worse, do something.

Now the siblings sat together in the quiet and watched the fire take. Sky had her head on Buckner's good shoulder and Jewell was drinking a bottle of beer and Lucy was staring at the low flames as they began to eat into the pallet. They were almost on the other side of it all, but there was still the matter of the wolf.

"He'd still be alive," said Lucy, "if I just did what Ralph wanted."

"You did the right thing," said Buckner. "Even if it didn't work out in the end."

"That pisses me off, too."

"What does?" Jewell asked.

Lucy picked up a pebble out of the dirt and tossed it at the fire.

"The fact that Mom was right."

"Right about what?"

This came from Jewell, who wiped at her mouth with the back of her shirtsleeve.

"Everything. I think she might have been right about everything at the end of the day."

"You're going to have to spell this out," Jewell went on. "Because there's no way you meant what you just said."

"I'm flabbergasted," said Buckner. "Speechless."

Lucy had not moved her eyes from the fire.

"I used to think when things went wrong it was because Mom made the wrong choice. I mean, right up until the day she died I thought that. Maybe I'm just trying to justify it to myself because of the wolf, but—"

"It's not your fault, Lucy," said Sky. "It's Darnette Lewis's fault."

"There can be more than one person at fault. And I am at fault, but what I'm saying is that I don't think what I did was wrong. That's the thing about Rhoda that used to drive me crazy, how she could be so sure of herself even when everything went to shit. And this went to shit, you guys. I mean, good Lord, it went sideways."

Jewell held up her left hand and measured an inch with her thumb and forefinger.

"Little bit," she said.

"The wolf is dead and Darnette got rich and got away with it all, but I think I would have done it the same way all over again. I really do."

"So, not only was Mom right," Jewell said, "but now you're worried you're turning into her?"

"In some ways, yes."

The fire grew with a little push of air.

"We all agreed to it, Luce," said Buckner. "We were in this one together."

"That's right," said Jewell. "And you know what wouldn't have happened if you didn't do what you did?"

"What's that?"

"Delos. He never would have found his way here."

"That's true," said Buckner. "That is one thing we know for certain."

"Funny thing is," Jewell said, "he wound up using the beau geste effect to perfection."

Sky took a drink of her beer.

"What the hell is that?"

"I've been reading about wolves. Doing a little research, and there's a French term for when a small group of wolves will shift the pitch in their own voices to make it seem like the pack is bigger than it actually is. They do it to intimidate adversaries. The translation is 'a noble but futile gesture.' That's exactly what Delos did. He just pretended like he was part of a pack to protect himself. In his case, it turned out to be true."

The siblings and Sky were quiet and sat with what Jewell had said. The fire churned and a big piece of pallet broke and rolled down to the edge of the pit and began to blacken and smoke.

"You should put that in your article for the website, Lucy," said Sky. "I didn't know wolves did that. That is cool as shit."

"Did you read my article?"

"She can quote it chapter and verse," Buckner said. "She's always fighting people on Facebook about it, too."

Lucy put a hand over her heart.

"Thank you, Sky."

Sky held up her fist in solidarity.

"It's a good article and people need to read it to know what's what."

"I actually had a whole paragraph written about it," said Lucy. "But I took it out because it would just scare people even more. How intelligent they are."

"That sucks," said Sky. "But you're probably right."

"I know I'm right about that," said Lucy. "Unfortunately."

"Real hunters should have been on our side with this," Buckner said. "They should have spoken up. There's no honor in poaching. No fucking skill to it. Fair chase used to mean something to people, but not anymore."

"Some spoke up," Lucy said. "Just not enough."

Buckner rubbed his eye with the cuff of his shirtsleeve. He might have been crying, or it might have been the smoke.

"They took that wolf's own heart and used it against him," he said. "With that pup call."

Jewell picked up a stick and poked at the smoking piece of pallet.

"I mean, if you got wolves running roughshod and want to

hand out some permits, that's one thing, but one wolf, trying to get back what they had taken away? I'll never understand it."

"Thing is," said Lucy, "what killed that wolf, the way he answered that call, it's something most people just flat-out aren't capable of. We leave each other behind. We do it every day. We let people suffer and die all around us and we pretend we can't hear them. That wolf heard one pup call out in the dark and he never hesitated. He never even blinked."

delos

At night, on the property, I always keep my window open. I like the fresh air and I like to hear my cousins out on the porch in their rocking chairs.

Sometimes, I stay awake just to listen to their voices. They are soft and steady and every now and then I'll hear a little roll of laughter or one of them cussing out one of the others, and with the window open I can smell the pine trees, too, and feel the cool air when a breeze comes off the river. I like to think about all that oxygen, and how far away from Woodyard I am and how I'll never go back to a place like that. How I'll always be here, where there's so much air to breathe.

I wake up every morning to bird chatter and rustling leaves and there is always somebody around the property to talk with, or to just sit beside and listen to the forest with.

I still have nightmares sometimes that I'm back in Woodyard, or at county, and I wake up all slick with sweat and my heart going rabbit in my chest, but then I'll remember everything that happened and where I am and I'll feel so grateful and relieved that I can hardly stand it.

One night, I was listening to Jewell, Buckner, and Lucy on

the porch when I heard a sound like a wolf call. I thought for a second that it was from the television down at Buckner's trailer, that maybe Sky was up watching TV, but then another call came behind it and I knew it was from the hills.

Two short howls went back and forth and everybody on the porch shushed each other and got quiet and all their chairs stopped rocking and the floorboards stopped creaking all at once.

Then a third call came and it was a full-on howl and then another came on and it was at least two wolves calling out together, maybe more, and their voices were colliding with the echoes of the first sounds and rattling around the hills before they spilled into the pines and flowed down.

I ran onto the porch and Jewell and Lucy and Buckner were all standing looking out in the same direction and then I saw Sky come running from the trailer with Frog in her arms and we were all so happy but we could not call out to each other, not just yet. All we could do right then was listen, and we stood in a group on the porch edge and all of us were there when the howls came together to form a chorus and rose.

acknowledgments

Huge thanks to my extremely better half, Cassy, the best human that I know and an ace reader who has never once led me astray. Leo and Edie give my life more purpose than I know what to do with, and are my favorite people to do everything with. Lyssa Keusch is a brilliant, patient editor and the team at Grand Central has been a joy to work with at each and every step. Seth Fishman is a fantastic agent, and his superpower is his ability to get into the messy part of books and separate the wheat from the chaff—it is an invaluable and rare talent.

Meaghan Mulholland writes beautifully and incisively about wolves and was kind enough to sit down with me and teach me some things about these amazing animals. She also said *Fair Chase* was a great title for this novel if I didn't already have one. I did have a title, but I went home that afternoon and deleted it because she was absolutely right.

My mom is a spiritual savant who helped me understand a long time ago that life is a lot more than what it oftentimes appears to be. My brother and sister have helped keep me afloat for as long as they've been on the planet, and Spoon is a good dog with a big heart who always barks for a reason.

And finally, a huge and heartfelt thank-you to the booksellers at McClean and Eakin, Two Dandelions, The Boswell Book Company, and so many other fantastic humans who work to provide the space for books to live.